The Scout of Terror Trail

The Scout of Terror Trail

WALKER A. TOMPKINS

Sagebrush
Large Print Westerns

Library of Congress Cataloging-in-Publication Data

Tompkins, Walker A.
 The scout of Terror Trail / Walker A. Tompkins.
   p. cm.
 ISBN 1-57490-516-3 (alk. paper)
 1. Scouts and scouting—Fiction. 2. Treasure-trove—Fiction. 3.
Outlaws—Fiction. 4. Large type books. I. Title.
 PS3539.O3897S38 2003
 813'.54—dc22   2003020416

Cataloging in Publication Data is available from
the British Library and the National Library of Australia.

Sagebrush Large Print Westerns are published in the United
States and Canada by Thomas T. Beeler, Publisher, PO Box 310,
Rollinsford, New Hampshire 03869-0310. ISBN 1-57490-516-3

Published in the United Kingdom, Eire, and the Republic of
South Africa by Isis Publishing Ltd, 7 Centremead, Osney
Mead, Oxford OX2 0ES England. ISBN 0-7531-6927-4

Published in Australia and New Zealand by Bolinda Publishing
Pty Ltd, 17 Mohr Street, Tullamarine, Victoria, Australia, 3043
ISBN 1-74030-934-0

Manufactured by Sheridan Books in Chelsea, Michigan.

TO
HELEN AND AUBREY

FRONTIER FORT

BULLETS SHRIEKED out of a death-ridden evening and thudded viciously against the blockhouse-cornered stockade of Fort Adios. A rising wind stirred off the desert wind freighted with a doom chant blended from the savage yells, defiant oaths, and roaring gunfire of the outlaw horde ambushed outside.

For ten peril-packed days and sleepless nights the handful of desperate defenders inside the isolated frontier garrison had blocked the besiegers. Now, with the fall of twilight on the tenth night, the savage ring of white outlaws and Apaches led by the notorious Don Chirlo was closing in like a death noose on the bayed New Mexico fort.

Fort Adios was rich in stores of clothing, food, blankets, ammunition—stores which Don Chirlo's band needed sorely.

Up in the square lot turret which guarded the northwest corner of the garrison, Lieutenant Curt Thode toyed with the lever of his carbine and chuckled silently each time he saw a skulking enemy through his loophole.

Any other man in the fort would have pawned an eye for the sure targets he had seen out there in the dust and smoke that afternoon. But Curt Thode's trigger finger wore a traitor's stain.

Hinges squeaked on the quick trapdoor in the plank floor of the watchtower.

Thode wheeled, swabbing water from his dripping face as a heavy-shouldered young scout strained through the trap and deposited an oak keg of gunpowder

1

at the officer's feet.

"What's the powder for, Daley?" snapped Thode, watching the newcomer crawl to his feet. A finger traced a white arc in the gloom of the tower as the scout snapped a weary salute.

Deo Daley worked his lips as he struggled to form words out of the breath which wheezed from his laboring lungs. The ear-riving bass roar of one of the garrison's cannon jolted the air under the faces of the two men in the darkness of the bastion.

"Major Fletcher—just issued orders to set the place on fire if—we lose out tonight, Sir!" gasped the scout in a lull of the chattering gunnery which rippled along all four sides of the fort. "There's—a wagon train with womenfolks inside this stockade, you know. Can't let Chirlo's devils get us alive. Orders are to die fighting with sabers. If they get over the palisade—set fire to—"

A wild fear showed in Thode's eyes, and knots of muscle gritted in his jaws. Both signs of panic were screened from Deo Daley's eyes by the cannon smoke which filtered through an open loophole.

"I'm to relieve you now, sir," the scout continued. "Major Fletcher expects the showdown tonight. Wants you to rest."

Thoughts churned under Thode's scalp. He shot a terror-filled glance through the loophole at his side. Out there in the brush surrounding the fort, the outlaws of Don Chirlo were creeping close. The rush would come after the falling of darkness.

Thode himself only that afternoon had sent the secret signal which told Don Chirlo that the fort's defense was done for. But Thode hadn't counted on his dogged commander's last order. Death before surrender. Lead and steel. Then fire the fort.

2

"But—we can't burn the fort! We expect the cavalry back tomorrow!" protested Thode hoarsely. Desperation strained his throat as he saw the dark blot of Daley's form moving up to thrust a gun barrel through the loophole. "We can hold them one more—"

Deo Daley glimpsed a shadowy figure darting from boulder to ocotillo clump. He whipped a quick bead, squeezed trigger, fanned smoke aside and grinned without mirth. A skulking Apache had dropped kicking. First kill all afternoon from that tower.

"I'm only the fort's trail scout, sir," answered Daley, levering a fresh shell into the breech. "You'll have to ask the commander about burning the fort. He's distributed oil and powder to every blockhouse and barracks building in the garrison. Why let Chirlo get the loot he wants? Remember what he did at Fort Sunset?"

Remember Fort Sunset! Curt Thode seized the rusty iron ring on the floor, jerked up the trap, and planted his boots on the ladder leading into the bottom story of the blockhouse. Remember Fort Sunset? Indeed, Thode would never forget that massacre.

Thode had been the outlaw band's spy there, too. He had personally tipped off the famous outlaw chief, Don Chirlo, the scar-faced, when to pounce on that unsuspecting garrison in Colorado, a year before. Chirlo had slaughtered the inhabitants, looted magazine and food cellars and soldiers' quarters, and left only a heap of smoking ruins to tell the tale of his ghastly outrage.

Yes, Thode had been the one who had informed Don Chirlo when Fort Sunset would be left short-handed, even as Fort Adios now was. Thode had faked an escape with garrison records, which had won him his lieutenant's bars and a commission at Fort Adios.

3

Brrom! The big Hotchkiss cannon mounted near the blockhouse bellowed out with a roar that jolted Thode to the roots of his teeth.

In the whisked-out interval of red light, he caught a glimpse of the cool-nerved young scout who had replaced him.

Daley wore a felt sombrero with brim pinned up, Texas-style, in front. Its crown was banded with silken cords in the colors of the famous Fort Adios Eighteenth Cavalry.

His torso was clad in a close-fitting blouse of tan buckskin. Sewed to the sleeve was the crossed-sabers insignia of the Eighteenth Cavalry, United States Army, stationed at Fort Adios.

A heavy Frontier model Colt .45 was belted to Daley's slim waist. His trousers were his only other badge of military service—the blue of the Fort Adios troops. They had the familiar yellow stripe of the crack Eighteenth vanishing at the knee into leggings of fringed buckskin decorated with copper. Spurred moccasin-boots completed his outfit.

"Bah!" Mouthing an oath through his teeth, Thode jerked the trap-door shut against the sight of the wellknit young scout who had taken his place with the soldiers at the hopeless job of defending Fort Adios against the invaders from the badlands without.

Thode scrambled down the ladder and strode out of the dark blockhouse into the dusk. Lined at gun ramps along the stockade, gaunt-faced men, many with brown-stained rags about arms or heads, were pouring bullets through slots in the log walls.

Away from the blockhouse Thode stalked, his pulses galloping. In the open space between bastion and his quarters were clustered a huddle of prairie schooners, canvas covers bullet-punctured. An emigrant train which, luckily for them, had been inside the stockade filling water barrels when Don Chirlo had swooped down.

The stench of sweating flesh and fresh wounds smote the traitor's nostrils as he threaded through the wagons. Fumes of burned gunpowder rode the night air. The besieged fort was a garbage-dump of smoke and dust and rotting dead.

"If Daley hadn't replaced me up there, I could get out to warn Chirlo tonight!" the spy snarled into the gloom. "Don Chirlo would shoot me down with the other rats if he saw this place go up in flames, after I signaled for a showdown. I've got to think of a way to warn Don Chirlo."

Thode's face was as black as a gun bore as he strode along through the bar of shadow flanking the officers' quarters. Jerking around a corner, he stopped in his tracks as he collided with a hurrying figure.

He opened his mouth to rip out an oath, then clamped it shut as he looked down through a void of twilight upon a girl's fatigue-drawn face. It was the daughter of the grizzled old veteran Tex Garland, who had led the caravan of wagons to the fort.

"Oh, Irene," grunted the lieutenant, stepping back and adjusting his uniform. "I've been wanting to talk to you."

The spy's glittering black eyes rested on Irene Garland's pretty young face. The girl was a beauty, in spite of the exhaustion from the siege.

She wore a wide-brimmed Mexican sombrero adorned with felt balls. Her tanned face was framed in clusters of brown curls. The army man could not see the girl's eyes distinctly, but he femembered that they were the blue of a dew-wet larkspur, with the same fibers in their lovely depths.

About her throat swung a necklace of bear's fangs, the gift of an admiring Osage squaw along the trail. Her blouse was of soft doeskin, its pliable folds rich with twinkling beadwork, and caught at the waist with a web-woven belt and a silver buckle.

An agate-hilted bowie knife was sheathed on that belt, close to one buckskin-skirted hip. The divided skirt had two agate-buttoned pockets, and beneath their leathern folds were ankles booted in soft leather.

"You must pardon me, Lieutenant," she said, starting to pass him. "I am going for the coffee bottles. The commander says it may be the last time I'll ever make the coffee rounds."

Thode clapped her shoulder. His voice carried an edge like clanking sabers as he shot back:

"I saw your silver horseshoe-nail ring on young Daley's finger when he relieved me tonight! How did he get it? Did he take it away from you or find it or what?"

The girl laughed, and twisted from his grasp. " 'Or what,' I guess," she answered saucily. "I gave it to him tonight. "

Thode twisted on his heels, his face dark with rage. With a flutter of leather skirts, the girl was gone.

Snarling with anger, Thode made his way to the door of his private quarters. He noticed with a shock that a half keg of sootlike gunpowder had been dusted over the plank floor of his room as he slammed the door behind him.

The officer turned up the wavering flame in the lamp which guttered on a wall sconce by the floor. The uncertain glare revealed him as rather handsome, in a dark, Latin way.

6

Partly Spanish, his skin was swarthy and his hair as straight and glossy as lacquered thread. He wore heavy side whiskers to the level of his ear lobes, and his black-pencil-line brows had an Oriental slant which gave an evil cast to his narrow face. A narrow mustache followed the curve of his upper lip.

Thode dressed in the blue uniform of the Eighteenth Cavalry, with a belt supporting clanking saber in a nickeled scabbard. Spurs chimed on his shiny boots. His hat was stiff-brimmed and peaked of crown. A lieutenant's bars graced his sleeve—a mark of honor, earned by playing a Judas role at Fort Sunset.

"First, he outclasses me with the girl; then he relieves me just at dark so's I can't get out there to warn Don Chir—"

Suddenly Thode wheeled on his heels, snapping his fingers sharply as if an idea had suddenly formed in his head. He strode swiftly to his bunk, peeled off army blankets, and removed a leather bag from beneath his pillow, next to the straw-tick mattress.

His brown fingers worked swiftly, rummaging through the shaving articles, spools, buttons and knicknacks in the bag. Then the spy's black eyes gleamed wickedly as he drew forth a glittering glass bottle. Many times in Thode's treacherous, slinking career, knock-out drops had come in handy.

That night, they might save him from a desperate situation. A fiendish plan was rapidly assuming pattern in his poisonous brain.

Knuckles rapped softly on his door as he was in the act of patting down the blankets over his mattress.

Palming the bottle of white crystals, he strode over the pile of gunpowder on the floor and opened the door. Revealed just outside the threshold was the

7

smiling face of Irene Garland, burdened with a basket filled with corked bottles of hot coffee for the fighting men.

"Won't you come in a second?" invited Thode, his teeth flashing in a smile. "I haven't seen you all day. Sorry I was so rude just now. Guess I'm jealous of that tramp Daley."

The girl's fingers fluttered over the collections of bottles in her basket, withdrew one bearing Thode's initials, and handed it to him. He uncorked it, threw back his head, and gulped a long drink of the steaming, refreshing liquid.

"Deo is no tramp!" the girl defended Daley, stepping inside and seating herself on a stool as she waited for Thode to finish. "He—he's more famous than you are, Lieutenant Thode. He's the scout of Terror Trail—the only man who knows Terror Trail. All the emigrants want him to lead them across the desert."

Thode shrugged, picked up the basket of coffee bottles from the girl's lap, and set it on a paper-littered table. Seating himself on the table, he slid the basket over so that his body hid the bottles from Irene's line of vision.

"Famous? Perhaps. But I hate to see you wasting your time on—on a frontier scout, Irene. What's wrong with me?"

The girl lowered her head, studying her folded hands shyly. Quick as a quail's dart, Thode's glance shot down to the basket of warm bottles in the basket beside him. In the yellow glare of the lamp on the log wall above he sought for and found, among the initialed flasks, the one marked D. D.—Deo Daley.

"A fine time for love-making, Lieutenant—when we may never see the light of dawn again. Major Fletcher says Don Chirlo will slaughter us tonight. But even the women will draw sabers. And the fort will be destroyed so they won't get what they want—supplies."

Thode's eyes fixed on the girl's bowed head, but his flying fingers were gently uncorking Daley's coffee bottle, then the little bottle of knock-out drops. The glasses clinked together faintly as Thode poured the entire contents of the bottle into the coffee.

"Major Fletcher is scarin' you. The cavalry is due back tomorrow. We can hold out one more night—we've done it for ten."

Thode curled his fingers over the empty bottle in his palm, deftly pressed the wet cork back into the coffee bottle.

The girl looked up as the Army man eased himself off the table, tossed down the last of his coffee, and replaced his flask in the girl's basket.

"But our men are wounded, tired," the girl protested. "That's why we have to keep them awake with strong coffee every two hours. They are dead on their feet."

Irene broke off, shuddering. She stood up, picked the basket off the table, and turned to the door. Thode bowed her into the night.

"Hurry along, Irene! The boys at the loopholes will be needing that coffee tonight."

Thode closed the door on the sounds of battle. For a long minute, he stood staring at the bottle in his damp fingers . . .

Half an hour later, Curt Thode slid like a shadow into the door of the northwest blockhouse and groped his way up to the base of the ladder leading into Deo Daley's lookout tower.

His coming to the blockhouse had not been noticed. Every eye in the garrison was squinting through a loophole, from the commanding officer to the lowliest

9

orderly in the cook shack.

Shoving upward on the heavy plank trap, the treacherous lieutenant crawled out on the floor of the pitch-dark chamber, and eased the door shut. From under his military jacket he removed a coil of tough tent rope, and a bottle of whisky.

"Daley!" Thode's cautious cry was greeted with silence. If the young scout of Terror Trail was inside this ten-by-ten cubicle, he was either dead from an outlaw bullet or was—

A sulphur match flared in Thode's hand. The guttering flame picked out the form of Deo Daley, slumped against the wall, knees buckled beneath him, hands still clutching a Winchester.

As he knelt before the limp form, a quick examination informed the traitor that Daley was not dead or even wounded. The light winked out in Thode's fingers, but not before the lieutenant's nostrils had confirmed the fact that the dose of knock-out drops had put the scout to sleep.

"Lucky they were makin' the Java so strong it would float a bullet!" chuckled Thode, picking up his whisky bottle and uncorking it. "Daley never knew what he was puttin' into his stomach when his gal brought *that* bottle of coffee, I guess."

The pungent odor of corn whisky tingled Thode's nostrils, but he did not drink. Instead, he felt out with one hand until his palm rested on the unconscious scout's face. Then, prying open the lips, he wormed the whisky-bottle neck between Daley's teeth and poured strong liquor into his mouth.

That done, Thode carefully splashed whisky over the drugged scout's jaw and fingers. The cold feel of Irene Garland's horseshoe ring—a trinket which Thode had

10

coveted and coaxed for, but without success—goaded the blind jealousy which festered in the traitor's arteries, as he sloshed the whisky about the room. He finished by coiling Daley's fingers about the half-empty bottle.

"There! I guess the stage is set!" whispered the lieutenant, getting to his feet. "They won't smell k. o. drops on him now."

Working swiftly, Thode proceeded to knot one end of his rope coil to a pine-pole rafter. The rope he dropped under the eaves and outside.

Then, scaling the log walls of the blockhouse, the spy of Fort Adios climbed until he hooked his arms over the topmost log. The blockhouse had been fitted with overhanging eaves and an open space above the plate, so that in case flaming arrows were shot on the roof, they could be snatched off by climbing outside.

The opening served Thode's purpose, that night. A moment later, he was climbing down the logs outside, his hands tightening on the stout tent rope.

Using the rope for a support, Thode lowered himself noiselessly and with catlike speed until his boot soles touched the blockhouse roof. Still clinging to the manila cable, he inched his way down the steep shingles until he could lower himself over the edge of the blockhouse. Then it was a simple hand-over-hand descent to the ground outside the fort.

He glanced about nervously as he hit the ground. Rubbing his hot palms, he flattened back against the blockhouse, panting.

But he had nothing to fear, from the fort. The blockhouse was empty. The shortage of men had left it without a guard, and the loopholes had been barricaded. The only danger would be from the sentinel tower above. And Deo Daley wouldn't cause trouble, now.

11

The blackness of a Destruction Desert night protected him from being spotted by the palisade gunners. If only some lurking outlaw didn't drill him by mistake—

Curt Thode lowered his head and sped out into the bullet-tortured night. Even as he gained the first thicket of mesquite brush, a dark figure leaped out upon him and a gun-barrel prodded the breath from his lungs. Thode's arms groped aloft.

"*Manos altos!* Who ees eet?" A gutteral peon voice hurled the challenge through a stench of foul breath.

Thode gulped a reply: "Lieutenant Thode. Don Chirlo's *compadre*. Quick. I have a secret message for your chief. Take it to him at once."

The outlaw pulled the army man back into the mesquite brake, scratched a match on his bandolier, extinguished it after a quick once-over of the spy's haggard face.

Thode lowered his arms, fumbled in a brass-buttoned pocket of his cavalry jacket, and pressed a folded square of paper into the Mexican's sweaty palm.

"You wait, *señor*. Don Chirlo mebbe wish so to see you, *si*," grunted the Mexican, turning and vanishing into the murk.

Curt Thode burrowed into the shelter of the thicket and flattened on the sand. As his eyes became accustomed to the darkness he saw that every stalk of saguero, every boulder, every defile and sumac-tufted dune sheltered one or more outlaws. Every man as tense as a steel spring. That meant one thing—they were awaiting Don Chirlo's signal to charge the fort.

In his mind's eye, Thode could see the hastily penned scrawl he had written in the secrecy of his private quarters.

"Don Chirlo: Do not attack the fort tonight, or commander will destroy all supplies. However, I have a better plan. Inside the fort is a wagon train stocked with the supplies you need—clothing, food, guns. Intended to stock a pioneer store farther west. It will resume its way along Terror Trail when you leave. So tomorrow when you see cavalry coming, pretend terror and flee. Then you can attack the wagons somewhere along Terror Trail and get your loot. If you attack the fort tonight, fort, wagons, and supplies will go up in smoke and you will gain nothing. Otherwise, you gain everything."

Long, tense moments the treacherous cavalry officer waited, his heart hammering his ribs, sweat oozing from his pores. Then he heard a movement in the blackness, and out of the gloom came a towering figure whom he recognized as Don Chirlo, king of bandits.

Clad in black velvet vest and bell-bottomed Spanish trousers with glittering silver trim, Don Chirlo was as vain as he was cruel. His face seemed to have been carved out of mahogany, then streaked and laced with puckered scars of knife and bullet and fist. "*Chirlo*" means "scar-face" in Spanish, and the name fitted the outlaw.

"Ah, my frien', the spy, Lieutenant Thode!" the outlaw chief greeted him, as Thode leaped to his feet, trembling in the presence of the great long rider. "I receive' your message. Deed you not know a dust storm ees come soon? Ideal night for attack."

"But the bull-headed *commandante* has scattered gunpowder all—"

"I know, I understand," cut in Don Chirlo, grinning savagely for a moment.

Then suddenly his face hardened into a horrid mask of rage, and his huge, talonlike hands shot out to seize Thode's arms with a grip that threatened to crush the bones.

"I weel not attack Fort Adios tonight, *Señor* Thode!" gritted the bandit leader, his mouth close to the spy's ear. "I weel wait an' attack the wagons on Terror Trail. But eef you lie—beware!"

Chirlo released one hand and his spikelike fingers rocked Thode with a vicious, stinging slap to the cheekbone.

"Eef theengs go wrong—eef these wagons, they no have loot"—Don Chirlo's face contorted with spine-freezing grimaces—"I weel cut out your spy's heart, *señor! Cut out your heart!"*

Thode backed away.

"Bah! Begone, *Señor* Thode. Back to your fort before they discover your absence, and I lose a spy. And remember—"

Thode did not wait for the outlaw to repeat his warning. Head spinning blindly, he was gone, headed for the fort at a run.

The blackness of death shrouded him as he made his stealthy way to the blockhouse wall. Spurred by terror, he scaled the rope, pulled it up behind him, straddled under the eaves and dropped down into the bastion. Quickly he untied the rope from the rafter above.

His tongue stuck to the roof of his mouth, as he noted that the body of Deo Daley was gone. Had they discovered his absence also?

Sick with fear, Thode ducked down the trapdoor, tossed his rope into the pile of stores in the dark blockhouse, and slipped outside to lose himself in the shadows of Garland's wagons. His beady eyes were

14

quick to notice a group of men by the guardhouse across the square, yelling and waving their arms frantically.

A running woman, bearing bandages and water to some wounded fighter, bumped into Thode in the darkness and fell sprawling against a wagon tongue. He picked her up roughly, rasped out a question:

"What's all the racket over by the guardhouse? Why aren't those men at their posts?"

The woman picked up the gauze and canteen. She was sobbing.

"There's been—they found a sentry asleep at his post in this hour of crisis!" she wept, leaning against his uniform. "It was young Deo Daley, the scout of Terror Trail we all liked so well. Major Fletcher himself went up there to—to take ammunition to the bastion, and found him there, drunk. Drunk! Dead drunk, when our lives depended on him most. They are taking him to the guardhouse to face a court-martial—if we pass through this night alive!"

The woman gasped through her tears as she saw a queer laugh expose Lieutenant Thode's teeth. Still laughing, he lurched off through the gloom, like a madman. Laughing, instead of swearing . . .

COURT-MARTIALED

EXECUTION DAY! The sullen *thub-thub-thub* of booted feet slogged echoes against the stern pointed-log stockade of Fort Adios. Overhead the last stars of a spent night were withdrawing from a graying sky as dawn brushed rainbow colors across the east.

Tramp-tramp-tramp! Men were mustered out two hours before reveille on execution days.

Even now, the scout of Terror Trail could hear the rhythmic thud of the platoon selected from the Eighteenth Cavalry to be his escort to the fatal wall.

Keys clanked in the grated door of the stone guardhouse. The jail corporal, sober-faced, nervous, unlocked Daley's cell and motioned toward the outer door with a nod.

"Sorry, kid," muttered the corporal, an old soldier himself. "We're all sorry. Even of stone-face Fletcher hisself. But that's the way with liquor. Makes a man crazy."

Daley smiled grimly. He strode outside. Took in with a quick glance the double file of uniformed soldiers, rifles on shoulders, awaiting him. A living man's pallbearers!

"March!" Out of the morning darkness came Lieutenant Thode's crisp command.

With two guards at either elbow, Daley fell in step as the platoon marched across the square of the fort. Executions always took place at the gates.

The Eighteenth Cavalry riders were away from the fort again. Daley was glad of that—glad that his friends did not have to see him die in disgrace, for a thing he

16

had been unable to fathom.

The cavalry had been called to the Lonely Valley settlements to the eastward, where it was reported Don Chirlo's gang was planning an attack.

"Platoon, halt!" Again Thode's brisk order, and the moving columns thudded to a stop, parallel to the fort's western stockade. Immediately in front of them were the huge swinging gates.

"Advance the prisoner to his position."

Daley licked his lips. At any rate, Thode was losing no time. So much the better. The endless waiting, waiting, was torture which would make death a welcome relief.

The two guards at Daley's side marched their prisoner to the wall. He had seen other men dragged there, sobbing, kicking, swearing. Some had to be tightly bound and propped against the wall. Daley matched his guard's stride, and turned to face the squad of soldiers of his own accord.

His hands were placed behind him. Handcuffs clicked. Another pair of manacles were snapped about the links and locked to a heavy ringbolt in the gate. This to keep him from bolting frantically at the last minute, in case his iron nerve snapped.

As the darkness thinned before advancing dawn, Deo Daley saw a new pine coffin outside the stockade and something else—a stack of twelve Springfields, on the parade ground in front of the platoon. All but one of them were loaded. That one had a blank shell. In that way, every man would think that he had pulled a harmless trigger.

Daley's guards took their places with the platoon of soldiers. The young scout, back to the west gate of the fort, fixed his eyes on the commanding notch of La

17

Cruz peak, over which the sun would lift to seal his doom in a very few clock ticks. Already, the horizon was blindingly crimson.

"Platoon—count off!"

Mechanically, the men began counting, from one to twelve. Many voices were mere whispers. Others croaked with defiance. Some openly sobbed. Deo Daley was popular, no matter what the verdict of the army court.

"Men with numbers four, six, and eight, march two paces forward!" commanded Thode, fingering his saber hilt nervously. His thin lips moved as twelve men, of the numbers designated, came forward.

"You are to comprise the firing squad. Advance, and select rifles from the stack." Thode's voice held an edge of triumph.

A movement in the dawn-lit shadows to one side gave Daley a chance to tear his gaze away from the spectacle of men selecting rifles—guns meant to plunge him into eternity. Friends of his; men he had played cards with, joked with, slept with, fought beside.

The moving shadow materialized into the commanding figure of Major Fletcher, highest authority of the garrison. Was he bringing a reprieve? But no. His presence was merely customary at an execution. As quietly as possible, Fletcher took his place.

Thode was coming forward, a black scarf billowing in the cool morning air. Daley straightened, scowled as he saw the leering traitor come to a heel-clicking halt before him.

"Remember—the horseshoe-nail ring is not buried with you!" taunted the officer in a steely whisper, as he lifted the scarf to blindfold the prisoner. "Spoils to the victor—"

18

A flood of panic swept through the young scout, as the black scarf shut off his vision. Then he calmed himself.

He could hear Lieutenant Thode striding away to take his post beside Major Fletcher for the firing orders.

"Arms—*ready*!"

Springfield pieces rattled as twelve stone-faced men, shoulder to shoulder, clutched rifles with sweating palms.

"Squad—*aim*!"

Daley pulled his eyelids open under the scarf.

Through its thick folds, he could see the dawn-flame in the east.

Twelve army Springfields were leveled at the stiff, defiant figure of the scout of Terror Trail, there on the gate of Fort Adios. A pink sheet of light spread and brightened over the garrison, as the dazzling rim of the sun poked over La Cruz peak.

Curt Thode broke his smile of fiendish triumph to frame the order which would press a dozen deadly triggers. But the sound stuck unvoiced on his very lips.

A rattle of pounding hoofbeats rang out on the dawn-hushed air! Dust boiled above the level of the stockade gates. And out of the stillness of death that had made room for the crack of twelve rifles, came the voice of the sentry posted in a blockhouse tower:

"Halt! A rider at the gate! Halt!"

Thode's ringing command to *"Fire!"* went unheeded in the uproar as a trembling group of men were forced to lower their rifles with gasps of terror as men flooded across the danger zone, following Major Aubrey Fletcher as he ran for the stockade gate, jerked down the heavy bar, and hurled open the side opposite the one to which Deo Daley was manacled.

19

Into the fort square lurched a blowing, dust-covered pony. Its sides dripped sudsy foam. Flanks dribbled blood. Eyes were red-shot, nostrils flared. A horse with a bursting heart, its knees wobbling from the killing exertion of a grueling ride.

Astride the reeling animal was a homespun-clad figure whom the soldiers of Fort Adios recognized instantly as the driver of a Tex Garland prairie schooner.

Even as they saw the horse stagger to a halt before the commander of Fort Adios, the rider pitched from the blood-smeared saddle into the major's arms.

"Don Chirlo's gang—attacked—wagon train!" gurgled the dying messenger, blood bubbling from a huge gunshot hole in his chest. "Trapped on—Fishhook Bend—four days out Blizzard Bluff—doomed—"

SUICIDE CHANCE

LIKE A PICTURE suddenly coming to life, the stiff files of Fort Adios cavalrymen broke ranks, clattering boots blending with jingling spurs as they gathered in a tight ring about the fallen horseman.

Gently, Major Fletcher lowered the red-soaked body to the ground, ripped open the woolen shirt. Rib fragments were exposed in the gaping wound. Protruding from the messenger's thigh was the broken-off stub of an Apache arrow.

"But our troops are away. We—we can't send any men to their rescue now!" gasped the commander, looking up at the sober circle of faces pressed about. "We thought—Don Chirlo was far away at Lonely

Valley. Our troops have gone there."

The soldiers bowed their heads, realizing the awful truth of the major's words.

The Eighteenth Cavalry was gone, leaving only this handful of men at the fort. Enough to defend it from attack, but not enough to send out against a powerful band of Don Chirlo's killers. Fletcher would not expose the garrison to such a siege as it had just pulled through.

The wounded man was gasping. His foam-flecked lips struggled to form words. Someone dropped whisky from a bottle on his mouth, and the fiery liquor seemed to revive him.

"Tex—Garland has wagon train—on edge of high cliff—overlooking river!" gasped the teamster thickly. "Could hold off—Don Chirlo—mebbe two days—but ammunition—running low—"

The major bent low over the dying man.

"Do you think, if we could get ammunition to the wagons, that they could keep Chirlo's gang at bay until I can recall my troops and rush them to their aid?" the officer questioned.

The messenger's eyes flickered shut. Opened again, their surface suddenly blazing. His lips moved, in a faint whisper:

"I—mebbe. Ammunition supply—nearly gone. Hurry—"

A spasm of coughing racked the wagoneer's body. With a long, quivering sigh, the form relaxed forever.

There was a lengthy silence, broken only by the mournful cry of a day-greeting *chacalaca* bird in some nearby clump of Spanish bayonet. A breeze whistled faintly through the pointed tops of Fort Adios's stockade wall. A soul had just taken wing.

Major Fletcher got to his feet, shoulders squaring with military woodenness. His burning eyes swept the crowd of sober-faced cavalrymen grouped about the corpse.

"Men, you are all familiar enough with the cliffs at Fishhook Bend to know that Tex Garland's wagon train is doomed," began the major, his spade beard quivering. "He is trapped at the base of Blizzard Bluff, overlooking the Rio Torcido. Retreat is impossible."

A sergeant spoke up, his voice husky in the quiet. "If he's cornered on the cliff's edge, he only has to hold off Don Chirlo from one side, sir. He could stand off an army for—"

The soldier broke off as Major Fletcher lifted his arms.

"Men, my duty cannot allow me to leave this fort open to a similar attack to the one it suffered two weeks ago," thundered the commander. "And it would be wasting men's lives to send them against Don Chirlo unless we were equal to, if not superior to, the ambushed forces of the outlaws. But Garland's men need ammunition, if they are to survive until I can get my troops there."

The army man paused, glancing down at the corpse below him.

"I am not going to give orders in a case like this!" cried the grizzled old warrior, taking a deep breath. "But if any man cares to gain heroism by taking a " suicide chance, let him volunteer."

There was a moment's silence, broken by Lieutenant Curt Thode's oily tones: "Volunteer for what, Major Fletcher?"

Fletcher grinned above his spade beard. "Volunteer load his saddlebags with ammunition. Ride to the Rio

22

Torcido. Break through the ring of Don Chirlo's bandits. Get that ammunition into Tex Garland's hands!"

Suicide chance! Curt Thode smiled to himself and stroked his thick sideburns as he glanced about at the men. Faces went hard and strained. Eyes crawled to avoid meeting the commander's stony gaze. They all knew what a suicide chance it was. Sure death!

"Very well!" The commander's voice held a tinge of regret. "It is no reflection upon the courage of any man here that he does not care to risk his life in a foolhardy, hopeless venture. But the picture of women and children serving as Don Chirlo's targets—"

"Major Fletcher!" Out of that panting press of men jammed about the dead messenger on the very threshold of Fort Adios, came the ringing, defiant cry. Of one accord, the men jerked about, and a little aisle spread to part the group as Major Fletcher turned slowly, to stare straight at the owner of that voice.

The words come from the blindfolded man who stood manacled to the heavy ring of the stockade gate. The man who a brief moment before had steeled himself for the shock of tearing lead. Deo Daley, the Scout of Terror Trail, was speaking!

"I volunteer gladly—if you will permit it, Major Fletcher!"

For a moment, the assemblage stood as if stunned. Then the commander tugged at his spade beard, strode forward, and jerked the black death scarf from Daley's face. The scout's eyelids widened, to reveal a pair of staunch blue eyes, cool with courage and determination. "But you—" Fletcher paused. "You are facing a firing squad, my man."

Daley tugged forward at his manacles, his voice

23

pleading. Before his eyes burned the vision of the girl who owned the silver band about his finger—a girl with eyes like larkspur petals.

"True, sir. I am a doomed man. Sentenced to die in dishonor for something I am unable to figure out. This—this is but another way o' facin' a firin' squad, sir. But if I win—if I get the ammunition through Chirlo's ranks an' into Garland's hands—I will have atoned my honor an' name before I face death. If I fail, your orders are fulfilled—I will be dead. If I succeed—"

Daley's gaze snapped to Thode, and the traitor shifted his eyes.

"If I succeed," the words tolled from Daley's lips, "I give you my word of honor to return an' face this firin' squad."

Moisture glistened on lashes that had not known tears through the strife of forty border campaigns, as the grizzled old commander clapped a firm hand on Daley's shoulder.

"Do not say that your death is my desire, son," whispered the old veteran. "You—you are a real soldier, Daley. I accept this offer, although it is, for you, a poor choice. But to speed you on your way, to bolster your faith on this suicidal undertaking, remember this: If you save Garland's train, upon your return to Fort Adios you will face not a firing squad, but a *full pardon!*"

A rousing cheer rocked the dawn at Fort Adios, and every throat save one lifted in a joyous cry as an orderly unlocked the manacles from the hands of the scout of Terror Trail.

One face was black, one heart surly with hatred, as the young scout burrowed through the broken ranks of back-slapping, cheering cavalrymen and headed for the stable to get his horse. That man was Lieutenant Curt

24

Thode, officer of the firing squad.

"What's the matter, Lieutenant?" queried the major, turning to Thode after giving orders for the burial of the wagon-train rider and the disposal of his exhausted mount. "Aren't you glad the young fellow has a chance to clear his name before he musters out for the last time? He'll never get back alive."

Thode whipped up a salute mechanically.

"With your permission, sir, I shall accompany young Daley—as far as the bluff overlooking Fishhook Bend snapped the treacherous lieutenant. "I feel Daley plans to escape."

Fletcher scowled. His spade of a beard went stiff like wire.

"Very well, Lieutenant. Send a man for your mount. But mark you: I grant this only for the sake of military form, mind you. I would trust Deo Daley to the very end of Terror Trail, Thode!"

Thus it was, a half hour later, that two men galloped through the open gates of Fort Adios, bound across Destruction Desert to a stricken caravan's aid. One, astride his coal-black saddler, headed to a fate almost as positive as a firing-squad's bullets. The other, riding a government cavalry steed, riding at Daley's stirrup as a grim guard . . .

The following dawn was straining the New Mexico horizon with pink when Scout Deo Daley and his unwelcome escort reined their weary cayuses to a halt on top of the towering, blunt-knobbed formation called Blizzard Bluff.

The trip that had taken the plodding wagon train four full days to cover had been traveled by the two horsemen in less than half the time, not stopping at

25

night. The grueling ride had left its mark in the grit-caked lines of fatigue which crayoned the men's features. A grim race with death across trailless desert.

"I expected to see a heap o' burnt wagons, but this is almost as bad, at that."

They were the first words Daley had spoken to the military man since the pair had set out from Fort Adios, open hatred seething between them, putting the scout on the alert for a possible shot in the back—a risk which he never permitted for a second.

From the brush-matted crest of Blizzard Bluff, the two men were looking down over the Terror Trail badlands. Blizzard Bluff was girdled on its western base by the Rio Torcido, which resembled a rill of mercury between its blue, shady cliffs.

At one point the river made a hairpin turn to avoid the buttress of Blizzard Bluff. The point, sheered off in sharp cliff walls slanting fifty feet from rimrock to river, was Fishhook Bend.

An appalling sight greeted the eyes of the two trail-weary riders as they leaned over their saddle horns and peered down through the mists of a newborn day.

Tex Garland's huddle of eight wagons, two of them overturned in flight, were jammed in a half-circle in the far corner of the bluff, at the brink.

Little puffs of smoke spurted from the trapped wagons now and then, to be whisked away by the same breeze which carried the bark of distance-muted shots to the two men on the bluff top.

Out of gun range below, at the base of Blizzard Bluff, Daley could see the camp of Don Chirlo and his outlaws—picked horses, a tent or two, bedding rolls. A breakfast campfire winked ruddily, twisting a thick spiral of blue into the morning chill.

26

In a fan-shaped spread before the wagons, hiding behind rocks, in washouts and chaparral, Daley could dimly see the antlike forms of the outlaws. Apaches and white men alike, all stationed at sniping posts, alert to cut down a glimpsed movement in the caravan. "It would be useless, even if I got the ammunition to 'em, to stand 'em off there in the open," Daley gritted, his eyes narrowing as he shaped his plans. "But if I could get 'em to that cave down yonder in that claybank—"

"What cave, Daley? Your job is to get ammunition through."

"Listen, Thode!" Daley spurred his black mount until his stirrup rubbed the cavalryman's. "You see that big bank they're trapped on? Well, it's a fifty or sixty-foot drop to the river. Current's swifter'n a greased shoat. But the water's scooped out a big cave directly underneath where they are, savvy. I've seen it a hundred times when I used to camp in that salt-cedar bosque across the river. If I could get Garland's folks down there, we could stand off those skunks o' Don Chirlo's until the troops get here."

Thode's swarthy features relaxed in a disdainful smile. He piled his hands on the saddle horn.

"Be sure you don't get drunk at the critical moment again!" he drawled. "And you'd better get going, because—"

Daley's eyes slitted, his mouth hardening into a knife-thin line. Suddenly his right wrist blurred, and Lieutenant Curt Thode found himself looking into the black bore of the scout's .45.

"I've swallowed enough o' your insults on this trip, Thode!" grated the frontiersman icily. "If I get those emigrants down that cliff wall an' into that cave, you'll

27

be there to see me do it. You savvy? Call that sassin' an officer if you like, but I'm bossin' the situation from now on. You savvy?"

Thode's face went chalky. His lips worked. Then color clotted his skin as his eyes danced from gun muzzle to Daley's face.

"If you live to get back to Fort Adios, the commander'll hear of this, Daley!" snarled the spy. "Lower that gun!"

The scout of Terror Trail wheeled his horse, but the unwavering Colt barrel remained trained on Thode's gilt-buttoned cavalry jacket, and the gun was at full cock.

"We'll see about that when the time comes, an' *if* we get back, Thode!" returned Daley shortly. "You insisted on ridin' here with me; now you're goin' to go with me *all* the way!"

Something in the scout's grim tone warned Thod of the peril of hesitating. Swearing at himself inwardly for having allowed the plainsman to get the drop on him, he turned his horse back down the sunny slope of Blizzard Bluff, Daley following close behind.

Down through the hackberry brush and cholla cactus the two wound their way. Daley kept his gun in hand.

Thode remained with face expressionless. Inwardly, he was praying that some cruising sentinel of Don Chirlo's, out rustling firewood, might witness this ride and shoot Daley out of his saddle, from ambush.

But Deo Daley, desert-wise and wary, was choosing a route which led around the base of Blizzard Bluff and cut the Rio Torcido at a point nearly a mile from the scene of the siege.

"We'll leave our hosses here, an' take a *pasear* along the river edge until we get to that cave at Fishhook Bend

28

an' look things over," explained Daley, motioning Thode to rein into an ignota-brushed draw. "Then, while you're roostin' there safe, I'll come back an' get to that wagon train somehow."

They hobbled and unsaddled their horses. Each taking a pair of ammunition-weighted saddlebags, the two men slid down a short cutbank and headed upstream, Thode in the lead, Daley close behind, gun still drawn, eyes alert for a suspicious move.

Their booted feet bogged in gluey sand. They clung to willows and waded ankle deep. They splashed through bars and clung to the mucky bank.

But an hour later, the long, twisting mile walk to skirt the base of the river's yellow cliffs was ended. They were standing on the broad shelf of clean gravel in front of the black maw of a cave which tunneled the cliffs of Fishhook Bend.

Fifty feet up, on the grassy rim of the cliff above, gunsmoke was scudding across the sky. They were directly under the bluff where the caravan was making its last desperate stand.

Curt Thode grinned. Don Chirlo would reward him richly, when the loot of Tex Garland's wagons was safely in his clutches.

Panting heavily, the two men entered the black depths of the cave. The floor of the cavern was littered with driftwood from flood waters that had receded months before.

"You scrape up some firewood—mebbe we'll have to boil water to make bandages for those poor cusses when we get 'em down here," ordered Daley, holstering his gun and tossing down his bags of ammunition. "I'll go now. You stand by when I start lowerin' those poor creatures down here with a rope. It's their only chance."

29

Grumbling under his breath, Thode made his way back into the dark cave, nursing a half-formed desire to whip out his own gun and fill Daley with slugs when the scout turned his back.

Going to the river's edge, Daley looked up at the overhanging wall above, and squinted up at the grassy ledge. If he could only attract Garland's attention—But that would be impossible, in the noise of the gunfire. And any mistake now might incite Chirlo to a storming, bitter attack.;

"Hiii!" A sudden yell from the interior of the grotto startled Daley, and he spun about, hand plummeting to his gun butt as he saw the lieutenant sprinting out of the shadows, pointing into the inky throat of the cavern.

"Come in here, Daley!" bellowed the cavalry officer, quivering with excitement. "I want you to see if I'm dreamin' or not!"

Frowning, Deo Daley snapped out his gun and followed Thode into the clammy depths of the cave. His every nerve and fiber was alert for a trap. What was the matter with Thode?

Had Tex Garland known of this cave under his battleground, perhaps, and tried to hide his wounded here? Or was Thode attempting a murder trick of some kind?

"I was scrapin' around hunting for tinder for a fire, when I discovered that!" cried Thode, thumbing flame from a match and pointing wildly down into the damp shadows. "My hands touched cold iron—and that's what I saw! Am I crazy? Did you ever see anything like that, in your years on Terror Trail?"

A sight of relief escaped Deo Daley. With a tired motion, he holstered his six-gun.

No, he had never seen anything so amazing as this

30

before, and he had seen many surprising things in the country around Terror Trail. But this was the most weird discovery of all.

Stretched at their feet was a human skeleton. Crooked green teeth leered in the guttery yellow flare of the match in Thode's fingers. The bones in themselves weren't unusual—merely some poor traveler who had starved, or had been drowned or murdered in this cave.

No, skeletons were commonplace along Terror Trail. But *these* bones were clad in the rusted mail armor and plate helmet of an ancient Spanish soldier! Armor complete to a brace of ancient Castilian pistols with peculiar, rough-knobbed ivory butts, and a Toledo sword in a rust-eaten scabbard!

THE HORSESHOE-NAIL RING

"NO, YOU'RE NOT DREAMIN', Thode," returned Deo Daley, turning to leave. "Centuries ago, a Spanish explorer named Coronado was through these parts. This poor cuss must o' been one o' those armored *conquistadores,* as they called 'em. Just think—he's been here for centuries, Thode. We're the first men that's ever had occasion to come into this cave, I reckon, an—"

"Look, Daley!" exclaimed Thode, lighting a new match from the dying one in his fingers, and kneeling beside the armored skeleton. "Here's an old arrow sticking through his helmet!"

But the bones of an age-dead Spanish warrior did not interest Deo Daley at the moment. Little did he' realize that Thode's chance find was to change the entire course of his life!

31

"Have a fire goin', see?" instructed Daley, his voice returning to its cold strain. "I got to get goin'."

Leaving Thode beside the rusty-armored bones, Daley hurried out of the dank cave and retraced the treacherous, slow-going mile, clinging to the lip of sand at the river's edge, until he could find a ledge on which to climb the gummy banks to rimrock and double back toward Fishhook Bend.

Plans were shaping themselves in his head as he crawled up a steep-pitched yellow bank, stood a moment sponging sweat from his face, and then looked to his .45 to make sure it was in order.

Then, on foot, he headed through the heavy mesquite and paloverde for the scene of the siege.

"Looks like Don Chirlo's restin' easy, not riskin' any men, knowin' that he's tricked the Fort Adios troops, so's they won't interfere!" grunted the scout, as he threaded swiftly through the cool blue haze of morning. "If there aren't too many men around that place, maybe this job won't be suicide, after all!"

But as Deo Daley crept within earshot of the ambushed outlaws, he saw that his worst fears were well founded. For a radius of one hundred yards in all directions from the wagon train, every rock or bush served as a hiding place for a gunman. To get through that ring of Apaches and outlaws would be impossible.

Closer and closer, the scout of Terror Trail crept. He was thankful that the frowning bulk of Blizzard Bluff threw this end of Fishhook Bend in purple shadow. He realized that Don Chirlo's men were enjoying this waiting game as a cat enjoys toying with a crippled mouse before devouring it.

Dropping to his stomach as he drew nearer, Daley slid forward around a nest of cold black rocks. Somewhere inside that splintered row of wagon boxes, somewhere under those beribboned, bullet-dotted canvas hoods, Irene Garland might be training a rifle sight on his skulking figure. But he would have to take the chance. He could not bring himself to think that possibly she was dead.

Brrang! Somewhere off to the right, a yelling outlaw sent lead crashing through spokes of an upturned wagon wheel.

One by one, he had bullet-bitten those spikes in two. With the coming of dawn, he had resumed his grim wheel-spinning game.

Indian arrows sang overhead to plunk with quivering feathered ends in the tattered canvas covers of the wagons. Daley shuddered as he realized what that meant. Chino's Paches didn't use arrows in desert warfare except for one purpose—to set fire to wagons. This meant that some Indian archer was getting in practice, before sending blazing shafts to destroy the caravan.

Burrowing his way under a tangled hedge of ignota brush, new sweat bathing his face, Daley suddenly tensed. A gasp whistled through his clenched teeth. For not five feet in front of him lay a feathered and paint-bedaubed Apache warrior! The arrow-shooter, on his stomach behind a block of ebony-dark rock!

If the Indian had heard Daley, he must have supposed he was an outlaw, taking his place on the firing front after a breakfast at Chirlo's camp. That had saved Daley's skin.

Drawing his .45, Daley shook off his vein-chilling dread and cocked the gun silently. On hands and knees, he crept ahead. One exploring palm slid across dew-dampened sand to disturb a nested horned toad. The little reptile scuttled away, rattling into a bed of dead

33

thistle poppies.

At the sound, the prone Indian turned his head curiously. Then the Apache's yawn clapped shut, and he seemed to freeze into a statue as his black eyes looked into a gun bore!

"Not a sound, you hear? Or it's happy huntin' ground!"

Before the Indian could recover from the first shock of finding the sultry-eyed plainsman on his very back, Daley had lunged forward to punch the cold gun barrel in the Apache's lower ribs.

The savage's throat worked, but a warning click from Daley's six-gun stifled the yell. The scout's flying fingers jerked a steel knife from the redskin's belt. The blade slashed the strap of the Indian's quiver of arrows, and a second later Daley had wriggled alongside the Apache and was whispering a mixture of Apache jargon, border Spanish, and Yankee into his ear.

"Keep quiet or you'll get six inches o' cold steel in your ribs, 'Pache!" snarled Deo Daley, worming the front sight of his gun between two of the Indian's ribs. "I got a scheme you're goin' to help me carry out with those arrows, savvy?"

With his free hand, Deo Daley drew a flint-tipped arrow from the Indian's buckskin quiver. With a cold smile, the scout ripped off the plume of dried creosote roots which would have formed a torch for a blazing arrow. Putting the arrowhead in his belt buckle, with a swift twist Daley broke the stone point off close to the root-wrapped shaft of reed.

Laying the beheaded arrow aside, while the sweating Indian looked on in terror, Daley fumbled in a triangle-shaped pocket of his buckskin blouse and removed a book of cigarette papers.

34

A stub of pencil from the same pocket was produced next, and, resting the paper against the black rock which hid him from view, Daley scrawled swift, terse words.

That done, still holding the quaking Indian in check with his cocked .45, Daley wrapped the cigarette paper containing his message about the shaft of the headless arrow. A quick wrap of threadlike root unwound from the arrowhead served to tie the paper in place.

Daley hesitated a moment, and then he shifted his six-gun into his left hand, put one finger in his mouth, and drew off the precious horseshoe-nail ring which Irene Garland had given him, that last memorable night of the Fort Adios siege.

"Reckon this'll let her know it isn't a trick," Daley grunted as he slipped the ring over the arrow shaft, sliding it down until it caught on the three feathers at the arrow's end. Then he handed the shaft to his trembling Indian prisoner and spoke again.

"See that closest wagon with 'California or Bust!' on it?" whispered Daley, forcing the Indian to look. "See the big hole in the front o' the wagon seat? Well, you shoot this arrow into that wagon, see? If it hits its mark, I won't kill you. But if it misses, you'll be gettin' picked over by buzzards come noon."

A quick prod of the Colt over the Apache's heart quelled the Indian's kindling flare of resistance.

Taut with terror, the Indian picked up his bow, and his brown fingers fitted the headless arrow to the bow. "On your knees, Injun!" ordered Daley, with a quick look about to make sure his presence was not discovered from behind. "Hit that bull's-eye, redskin—or it's taps for you!"

The Indian tensed the bowstring, lifted himself for a moment above the level of his rock ambush, released the arrow with a *twang*.

Brang! Out of the wagon which Daley had recognized as that of old Tex Garland came a finger of red fire, and the Indian archer flopped backward, with a lead ball splitting his nose.

But his last arrow had winged its way as straight as a beam of light—squarely into the puckered drawstring opening of Tex Garland's prairie schooner.

"Sorry, Injun!" grunted Daley with genuine regret, as he holstered his .45 and proceeded to remove the feather war bonnet from the dead Apache's head. "I would only have conked you with my hog-leg butt, if you hadn't got sniped this way."

Moving swiftly, Daley squirmed back in the shelter of an ignota hedge and commenced peeling off his blouse and belt.

Tex Garland lay flattened like a whiptail lizard on the splintery floor of his wagon bed. Cuddled along his whiskered cheek was the polished walnut stock of a big-calibered Sharps. Jabbed in his mouth was his perpetual black-lined corncob.

For twenty-four hours, the veteran had not closed his eyes in sleep. Daylight had been a nerve-sapping ordeal of sniping at darting red bodies out in the brush. Nights were tense with the strain of expected attack.

A sudden movement over to the right, and the man swung his rifle barrel through the knothole he was using as a firing point. Squarely between the beads of his rifle, the Texan saw the feather-bonneted head of an Apache, in the act of drawing a loaded bow.

Brrang! The weapon jolted Garland's shoulder. When the smoke sifted away, the Indian was gone. Instinct told the Texan he had scored a hit.

Something came whistling in through the drawstring-puckered opening in the canvas front of the wagon, bounced against the hickory rib of the cover, then fell with a clatter upon the sleeping body of Irene.

The girl stirred, opened panic-drenched eyes, and gasped. With a moan of apprehension, Garland wriggled about, as he saw an Apache arrow lying across the girl's chest. For a moment, the old man fancied he saw blood gushing from the end of the arrow. Then he noted that the shaft had no flint head on it, thereby creating the illusion that the arrowhead had buried itself in the girl's flesh.

Shaking her head to clear her brain, the girl sat up. As quickly, the old man shot out a hand and pressed her prone to the wagon bed once more.

"Steady, Irene! That's a brave gal, daughter. Can't risk our heads above the level o' our wagon box, you know."

The girl reached instinctively for the Winchester at her side. A sheepish grin parted her lips as she realized she had let her jaded nerves drag her into a moment's slumber.

"Look what just come in an' woke you up, daughter!" chuckled the old man, hoarsely, to cover her mounting confusion. "Alarm clock, Western style. A Injun arrow, with the head knocked off."

Rubbing her eyes sleepily, Irene Garland picked up the slender shaft which had roused her from her slumber where the monotonous shock of an exploding Sharps rifle had not. As she picked it up, a tiny flash of white light slid down the reed shaft, and a cold object lodged against her sensitive fingers.

Tex Garland was sucking match-flame into his odorous pipe, so that he did not see the quick flush

37

which spread across the girl's face. But he turned as he heard her gasp of amazement.

"Daddy! Daddy! *Look!*" cried the girl, sliding to her father's side. "See! Here on this arrow! It's the ring I gave Deo."

Garland's seamed old face sobered with puzzlement as he saw the girl lift the silver horseshoe-nail ring off the arrow—the ring old Tex himself had fashioned for her on her nineteenth birthday, the summer before. The ring she had given to the young plainsman at Fort Adios, the scout of Terror Trail.

"And—and look, Daddy—paper wrapped on the arrow. Maybe it's—"

With hands that trembled for the first time since her father's wagon had been attacked, Irene Garland unwrapped the tissue-thin cigarette paper from the Indian war arrow. In the dim half-light which ribboned down through the bullet-ripped cover of the wagon, she read aloud:

"Garland: Am in pile of black rocks near your wagons. Am coming out dressed like Indian. Let all wagons know so I won't be shot. Signal out of your wagon when coast is clear. DEO DALEY."

Garland shook his head in alarm. "It's a blasted trick o' Don Chirlo's to trap us!" he growled. "Young Daley's dead an' buried by now. No, sir! I'm shootin' any Injun I see."

Irene caught his arm. "No, Dad! It might even be Deo's ghost, but that's the ring I gave him! I'll make the signal!"

From about her throat the girl unwound a blue bandanna. Balling it in her palm, she threw it out of the hole in the wagon cover through which the strange arrow had come. The blue cloth billowed into a square as it settled groundward. Even before it vanished from Irene's sight, it was snatched and perforated by a vicious snap-shot bullet, proof of ever-present peril.

It was Tex Garland's turn to be astounded now. Hardly had the bandanna dropped to the earth, when over the black rocks outside the bayed ring of wagons leaped a half-naked figure, surmounted by a trailing brown-and-white bonnet of eagle feathers.

"*Yowww! Whooooooieie!*" Brandishing a rifle, yelling like a drunken maniac, an Apache warrior came dancing out on the sand, while a chorus of startled and protesting yells broke from the other ambushed outlaws. Was this redskin drunk? It was suicide!

Crash! Feathers went flying in a blurry shower from the Indian's war bonnet as Tex Garland and Irene lent realism to the hoax by triggering lead over Daley's head.

Zigzagging and leaping, a knife in one hand and the rifle in the other, the "Indian" came at a galloping run until he tripped on a dead ox just outside the half circle of wagons.

Clambering to his feet, still yelling wildly, the befeathered warrior climbed to the dead carcass's belly, hurled his knife in a foolish throw at the nearest wagon, and then staggered drunkenly between two wheels and inside the ring.

A rifle blazed inside a wagon. The outlaws who stared in open-jawed silence from ambush saw the man they supposed to be their fellow clutch at his chest, twist, and fall out of sight.

"Serves the drunken Injun right!" howled a throaty outlaw voice. "Who in hell give redeye to thet 'Pache, nohow?"

But the "dead Injun," his movements safely hidden by the ring of ox carcasses dragged just inside the arc of wagons, had miraculously come to life.

Shielding his body behind the dead animals until he got to Garland's wagon, Deo Daley climbed a wheel and a moment later was ducking over the seat into the prairie schooner. Clad in Indian war bonnet and trousers, he looked his Apache role.

"Deo! Deo!" Irene Garland was in the young scout's arms, her tears on his brown-skinned chest as he whipped off the Indian headdress and turned swiftly from the girl to the grinning old teamster. "I'm so glad, Deo—so glad! How did you ever—"

"Easy, Irene! I'll explain later," cried the scout, wasting no time. "How come you signaled me so quick? How about those other wagons? How many men you got left, Garland?"

The Texan's blue eyes filled with tears. His head drooped.

"Nary livin' soul, Daley. We're the last. Babies, women, old men—all dead. You can see why we're still alive. Plowshares."

Glancing about, Deo Daley saw why Tex Garland and his daughter were the sole survivors of the once large caravan. From his stock of freight, Garland had dragged a dozen shiny plowshares, under the cover of darkness, into this wagon.

The steel shares, overlapped side by side about the wagon bed, served as a perfect armor plate for the bullets which had splintered the oaken wagon-box sides until they resembled a nutmeg grater. More than one leaden pellet had cooled on the outside of those shares.

Deo Daley's first shock of horror at learning the gruesome fate of the men, women, and youngsters in the

40

other wagons was engulfed by his feeling of thanks—giving for the delivery of those who meant the most to him—the old Texan and his daughter Irene.

"Come on! There isn't a minute to spare!" snapped the scout of Terror Trail, as he swiftly outlined the position of the cavern under the Fishhook Bend bank. "Show me some ropes, Garland! When it gets a little more light, they'll charge you, for sure!"

Slashing a hole through the canvas cover on the inner side of the wagon hood, Daley made an opening through which he crawled outside, followed by Irene and the old man. Twenty feet away, over ground that was hideous with the grisly corpses of men and beasts, was the grassy edge of the bank overlooking the Rio Torcido.

Garland shuddered as he climbed into another wagon, turning over bullet-hacked bodies of defenseless women with murdered babies clasped in their dead arms. Out of the wagon he dragged a heavy coil of manila rope, which he made fast to a wagon bolster.

Daley took the coil of rope and, crawling on his stomach through the piles of dead inside the crescent of wagons, laid it on the bank brink and motioned Irene Garland and her father to crawl to him with all possible haste.

Bullets droned overhead, singing off steel wagon tires, ripping canvas to tatters, thudding sickeningly through dead bodies, chiming metallically off stoves and kegs, plowshares, and kettles.

"Come on! Irene first! Lieutenant Thode's down there to help you. He's got a fire in the cave."

Tying a rope loop under the girl's arms, Daley swung Irene over the edge, and in a moment he and Garland were lowering her down the overhanging, fifty-foot bank of the Rio Torcido.

41

Minutes later, the rope came up free, and Daley was bracing his legs against an ox's quarters as he lowered Tex Garland, swinging like a clock pendulum, to the mouth of the cavern.

Leaving his rope dangling over the cliff edge, Daley ran to the nearest wagons. They might be trapped in that cavern for days, until the Fort Adios troops arrived; he had to make precautions.

A moment afterward, he was pitching boxes of dried fruit and venison over the grassy hem of the cliff. This he followed with a pair of blankets, some canteens, and extra guns. Then, returning to the wagons, he proceeded to break open a keg of oil.

Wrapping some dead woman's shawl about an ax handle, Daley plunged the swab into the oil. That done, he carried the keg from wagon to wagon, splashing oil over the canvas covers and tinder-dry wooden boxes, always keeping behind the barricade of ox carcasses, to avoid an outlaw bullet.

When he had finished his circuit of the covered wagons, he crawled back on all fours, scratched a match on an axle, and fired his oil-soaked ax-handle torch.

A minute later, eight prairie schooners were blazing. Tumbling black smoke corkscrewed into the New Mexico sky, covering another of the many unknown, unmourned tragedies of the West.

Baffled cries of fury rang out from the outlaws ambushed along the banks of Blizzard Butte. They leaped from cover and charged forward, risking death as they stormed the raging flames of the caravan's funeral pyre.

But they were not quite quick enough to see the half-naked, Indian-like scout of Terror Trail as he ran swiftly to the bank's border, lowered himself over the brink, and slid hand over hand down the fifty-foot drop of manila rope, to drop light as a cat on the gravel shelf which sprawled from the cold throat of the cave.

THE SPANISH PISTOLS

NIGHT GROPED DOWN off the Rocky Mountains to bury the washed-out cavern in Fishhook Bend's clay walls with sooty blackness.

Down in the cavern, nightfall deepened the anxiety which petrified the hearts of four mortals. Would Don Chirlo attack them, here on this driftwood-littered floor of the cavern?

A watch was maintained constantly. Tex Garland was taking his turn now, outside the cavern's mouth. Alone with his thoughts, the brooding old veteran chewed his corncob stem and acknowledged total defeat for the first time in his sixty-odd frontier years.

Friends slaughtered during a brief but fatal siege. Wagons gone. Savings of a lifetime reduced to ashes. But he was glad Don Chirlo's band would not profit by their attack, thanks to Deo Daley's quick thinking.

Garland knew that the chance of escape from this cavern was remote. He knew the vengeful Don Chirlo was even now up on the slope of Blizzard Bluff, plotting revenge. But at least the Scout of Terror Trail had provided food, fuel, blankets, and ammunition with which to make a last desperate stand against the outlaw horde.

Inside, seated about a guttering fire of damp drift, stark terror gnawed at the craven heart of Lieutenant

Curt Thode. Fear of Don Chirlo; not of his bullets, but of his rage.

Everything had gone wrong for Don Chirlo. And the vicious half-breed outlaw king had promised to cut out Thode's heart if things did go wrong. What would Chirlo think of Thode's presence here in the very camp of the enemy? He could never explain that.

Irene Garland, arms folded on crossed knees, stared into the warm coals of the campfire and tried to keep her thoughts off the bones of the Spanish caballero molding inside a husk of rustling armor, just back in the inky shadows. A ghastly mystery, that.

Deo Daley, looking like an Indian as he sat with naked back to cave wall snatching a few moments' rest from his vigilance, let his eyes rove from Irene's fire-splashed features to the pair of knobby-handled Castilian pistols he held in his hands—the guns he had taken from the dead Spaniard's belt.

All afternoon, Deo Daley's thoughts had been on something he had found on those ancient guns, with their clumsy flintlocks, their huge, uncomfortable, knobbed ivory stocks yellowed with age. The barrels were silver-plated, and in the tarnished metal Deo Daley had discovered, on his first curious inspection of the ancient weapons, a line of Spanish words etched along the side of one massive barrel.

"Rico es que tiene el secreto de estas pistolas." Daley could read Spanish fluently, from a lifetime along the bitter Mexican border. But the translation of that mystic sentence puzzled the scout of Terror Trail even more than the original words: *"He is rich who possesses the secret o f these pistols."*

A vast mystery was couched in those words, Daley was sure. The very presence of an armored conquistador's bones in this forgotten cave revealed some drama-packed mystery of the age-old past. These pistols possessed the key to that secret—but what was it?

The guns were centuries old. The bones back there in the shadows were centuries old, and only by a queer trick of fate had they been discovered at all.

Midnight passed. Curt Thode replaced Daley once more at the eternal watch at the cavern mouth. With the passing of hours, the gnawing terror grew in Thode's heart. Could he escape? One look at the inky gliding surface of the Rio Torcido quelled a half-formed impulse to escape by the river.

Besides, Don Chirlo had undoubtedly scattered guards along the banks above. Thode knew Chirlo well enough to realize that the cruel bandit would not permit them to escape with their lives. And if he found his spy, Curt Thode, among his enemies—Thode shuddered as he recalled Don Chirlo's last fierce threat.

A sudden cry from within the cavern, and Thode spun about with a violent start. Then he saw the black outline of Deo Daley in his Indian garb, standing beside the campfire inside, bending over Irene and her gray-bearded, pipe-smoking father.

"I've got it! I've found it! The secret of these pistols!" the scout of Terror Trail was crying. "Garland, if we aren't too late, these pistols will make us rich! *Rich,* I tell you!"

Thode had never seen the ice-nerved young scout excited, in all the time he had known Deo Daley. But now the man was panting heavily, chattering excitedly as he held the two Spanish guns to the light. Creeping forward, but keeping in shadow—Daley had ordered him to keep a strict guard—Curt Thode saw that Daley had removed the queer-knobbed ivory stocks of the two old guns.

"Did you ever hear of the Castle of Thieves—the Alcazar de los Ladrones?" Daley was shouting, as he thrust forward the two ancient pistols under the old wagon-driver's startled nose. "No? But of course, you are from the East. Then listen, Garland. It's a wild story, Irene. That old Spaniard back in the cave here knows it, but listen close. If we can get out of here alive, we're rich! Do you hear? These pistols will make us rich as kings!"

And a wild, uncanny story it was, the tale that Deo Daley unfolded, there in the clammy depths of the Rio Torcido's cavern. A story to baffle the most vivid imagination! A legend that had been born centuries before, and that had grown from constant retelling around prospectors' fires, by drunken cowboys in frontier saloons, by outlaws along the hunted out-trails of the grim, wild West.

A spectral and weird story indeed, that of the Castle of Thieves. Listening, Irene Garland agreed that it outclassed the sum of all the tales of lost gold mines and buried treasure in the entire West. The *Alcazar de los Ladrones!*

Absurd? Yes, but Deo Daley believed the story he told. So did Tex Garland, who was not easily fooled. And Curt Thode, the spy of an outlaw band? Yes, Curt Thode believed Daley's fantastic story. He listened closely, while Deo Daley talked.

Back in the 1500's, when Spain was pushing her explorations to the Pacific, conquering Mexico and exploring the Mississippi, a group of Spanish pirates and highwaymen followed the footsteps of Coronado and his

46

soldiers into the Southwestern badlands.

Led by a noted Spanish outlaw, Don Picadero, they were fleeing from the wrath of the crowned heads of two nations whose ships and colonies they had fleeced. Into the rugged wastelands they went, armored fighter of Spain, with trains of burros laden with gold and treasure of the Spanish Main!

Somewhere—legend had it that the outlaws never divulged the place—Don Picadero built a Spanish castle, where they stored their plunder of gold and armor and jewels. To protect their secret, Don Picadero decreed that the Indians who had helped to erect the castle had to die, so that its location would be unknown.

But the angry Apaches of antiquity descended upon the *Alcazar de los Ladrones,* and commenced a siege from which there was no possible escape. A few Spaniards happened to be outside the walls at the time, and they fled toward civilization. But only one lived to tell his story of the Spanish treasure house.

"That Spaniard raved deliriously for days on how his *compadres* had died o' thirst in the desert or had been attacked an' tortured by savages," Deo Daley was panting. "But before that Spaniard could tell the secret of Don Picadero's treasure castle, he died."

Thus, with the passing of decades, the Castle of Thieves had become a legend. White men believed it to be a myth, like the Fountain of Youth. Through centuries of time, the colorful fable persisted—a legend which had lured untold scores of prospectors to their deaths, hunting the lost Spanish gold.

"But, Deo, how does this story affect us? What has it to do with these guns you found on the skeleton?" asked Irene, as Daley paused for breath. "Was he from this treasure castle?"

The scout of Terror Trail shot a backward glance in the shadows, where the rusty bones lay. He nodded, grinned, went on:

"He was one o' those escaping pirates—yes!" shouted the scout. "And see—while I was fooling with these guns, trying to find out their secret, I took off these funny, bumpy ivory handles. And inside them—see the words carved there? It's Spanish. It says that the bumps on this handle form a relief map of the Terror Trail country—and where a jewel is set in the handle, there is the location of the lost Castle of Thieves. Don't you see?"

Garland leaned forward. Irene sprang to Deo Daley's side. Back in the shadows near the cavern mouth, Curt Thode forgot his terror of Don Chirlo, and strained traitorous ears, not noticing the lurking forms which gathered silently in the shadows outside.

Nested in the cup of Daley's palm were the two ivory stocks of the guns—four half-sections. Sections which, when laid together, formed a map—a relief map of mountains and buttes, rivers and mesas, leading to the *Alcazar de los Ladrones* and its treasure!

"See—this butte here, this lump on the gun stock shaped like a goat's head? That's Goathorn Mesa, fifty miles west o' here on Terror Trail!" exclaimed Deo Daley. "The jewel it speaks of is missing from its setting, but there is the little hole where it was."

Tex Garland drew at a cold pipe, his eyes glowing strangely.

"Then—then you recognize the bumps an' hollows on this gun stock as bein' them badlands o' Terror Trail, eh? Them scratches are rivers? An' you think you can find this lost treasure castle?"

The scout of Terror Trail opened his mouth to speak,

48

but at that instant there rang out in the cold depths of the ghostly cave an ear-throbbing gunshot.

Something hot grooved Daley's neck. Dizzy with bullet-shock, the scout turned, then gasped with terror. Flooding through the mouth of the cavern came Don Chirlo, backed by a wall of yelling Apaches and murderous outlaws!

Deo Daley shot out both arms and encircled the heads of Tex Garland and his daughter, crushing them earthward a trifle of a second before a wall of screeching lead coursed over them.

Ripping a blanket off the cavern floor, Daley flung it over the fire, plunging the grotto in darkness. Grabbing out during the split clock-tick before confusion exploded with a babble of bawling oaths and popping gunfire, Daley seized the pioneer and the girl and dragged them to one side.

"Thode was slackin' sentry duty—let 'em sneak up on us!" croaked Garland in a hoarse bellow. "We're done for!"

Outlaws, blinded by the gloom, were stumbling on tangled driftwood, sprawling over each other, screaming oaths.

" 'Wait!" came Daley's voice in Garland's ear. "Sneak along behind me. Got to run for it! Stick together!"

Daley in front, Irene in the center, Garland following, the three slipped forward, straight toward that screaming, oncoming stampede of fiendish murderers.

A groping body crashed into Daley. The scout lashed out an iron fist that crumpled an Apache jaw. Then the white man was hurling the limp, naked body out into the center of the rush. Five oncoming men stumbled on the form and went down, screeching.

49

By the light of a flaming six-gun, Daley saw a void of space ahead, and dived through, clubbing down a red-bearded crook with his .45.

Daley, half-naked in his Indian costume, passed unchallenged as he rubbed and squirmed against jostling bodies in the blackness, mowing down an aisle for Irene and the grizzled old veteran to follow.

Armed with a club and her bowie, Irene was accounting for herself. Skulls cracked and flesh wilted under the crushing blows of a Sharps rifle butt swung by Tex Garland.

The air was thick with the smell of sweaty bodies, scorching blanket, smoke and dust. Eardrums ached under the shots that chipped sandstone from the cavern roof. In the sirup-thick gloom, Deo Daley was fighting with fist and foot and clubbing gun barrel through the heart of the mêlée by the cave mouth.

Someone kicked off the smoldering blanket and swept a glowing wood chunk aloft. In a second, Daley had his bearings and was dragging the two Garlands outside the cave, his six-gun roaring a song of death, bullets thudding into collapsing outlaw bodies.

An instant later he was checking his trigger finger, as his gun swung to line its sights on a lurching figure who was dressed differently from the other attackers. The yellow-striped uniform of a U. S. cavalryman—

"Curt Thode!" Daley yelled, as the lieutenant drew closer. "You're to blame for this—sleeping on guard duty or whatever you did—but you'll have a chance if you keep by us—"

For a fleeting moment, indecision swept Thode's face. Then, perhaps fearful of falling victim to a stray slug, fired blindly by one of Don Chirlo's henchmen, Thode nodded agreement.

50

"Let's go—before it's too—"

Spinning, Daley headed for the river edge, yelling madly at the two Garlands as he swept them with him:

"Into the river, Irene! Dive, Garland! They got us!"

Four splashes went unheard as the mouth of the cave disgorged a dozen fighting, shooting men, each slugging at unseen bodies in the darkness, while the crook with the torch fought his way through the jam to get outside.

Neck deep in the swirling waters of the Rio Torcido, four heads came to the surface, twenty feet out in the sluggish eddies.

"Swim, Irene?" gasped Deo Daley, his half-naked body cleaving the water like an otter as he got an arm on the girl's shoulder. Off to the left, Tex Garland was blowing like a steer through a sopping beard, but keeping afloat, Curt Thode beyond him.

"Like a fish!" gasped Irene in reply. "Better help D—dad!"

Supporting the old man, Daley kicked and stroked out into the main current. The yelling outlaws were behind. Lights winked along the brush-furred cliff brinks above.

Bullets skipped across the water, but they were wild shots. Outlaws were swarming along the banks above and below, but they were fast dropping behind as the current swept the fugitives around a bend out of bullet range.

The current slowed down as they swept around another bend. Then they were hurled into the vortex of a whirlpool. Pads of foam clung to Daley's body as he looked about, eyes focusing in the starshine, picking up the black rim of the bank off to the left.

"Quick—ashore! We can't last in this water! Help me here, Thode!"

Helping the old man's failing strokes, Daley and the Army man fought through shallowing water until his moccasin-clad feet touched sandy bottom. Irene Garland drew herself to the bank a trifle of a second after Daley and Thode had dragged Tex Garland into the tules at the foot of a steep cutbank.

Hoofbeats drummed in the night. Frogs trilled nearby. Flaming torches gleamed afar. Don Chirlo's gang was in the saddle, sweeping down the slanting mesa from Blizzard Bluff, alert to guard the river bank for miles.

"We—we're lost! No hosses—" Garland croaked. Picking up the wet teamster by the armpits, Irene on his other side, Daley struggled up the cutbank, across a greasewood-dotted flat, and into the black maw of a draw. Five seconds later, two horses loomed magically in the star glow.

"Thode's bronc—an' mine!" explained the scout of Terror Trail to the astounded fugitives. "Cached 'em here yesterday afternoon, when he and I went up to the cave. Quick! You 'n' I'll ride double, Irene. No time to saddle. Fork Thode's horse, Tex."

Thus it was that two more horses galloped out of the draw into the very teeth of an advancing horde of outlaws, and mingled with the galloping horsemen until, twenty minutes later, they had worked to the outer edge of the murderers' stampede and had lost themselves in a barranca-gashed country which Deo Daley knew like a book.

And inside the waistband of the scout's Indian trousers were four pieces of knobby ivory and two Spanish pistols—keys to a long lost Spanish treasure! What he did not know was that Curt Thode had relayed the secret of the map to Don Chirlo, and that the bandit was already on the march.

On Destruction Desert next morning they met Major Fletcher and his crack troops of the Eighteenth Cavalry, fronted by the glorious Stars and Stripes—headed too late for Blizzard Bluff and an outlaw-destroyed wagon train.

Six rows of erect young calvarymen were drawn up in dress parade at Fort Adios that afternoon, mounted astride glistening war steeds. Flashing sabers lifted in a stiff salute as Major Aubrey Fletcher presented the smiling, blue-eyed young scout of Terror Trail, once again clad in his familiar buckskins and cavalry trousers.

"Not only are you fully pardoned with a clear name and restored honor on the records of Fort Adios," thundered Major Fletcher's happy voice, "but I hereby offer you a captain's commission in the United States Cavalry."

Deo Daley, standing at stiff attention before the proud ranks of the famous Eighteenth Cavalry, let his eyes stray past the horsemen to the open door of the headquarters cabin.

An old veteran of the Western trails stood there, trickling smoke ribbons through his salt-colored beard. At his side stood a beautiful girl in deerskins, her face radiant with joy and pride.

New hope burned in the eyes of the two, for out of the destruction of their dreams and fondest hopes had risen a new vision—a glamorous adventure promising as its reward a lost Spanish treasure castle, somewhere out there on the desolate reaches of Terror Trail!

"I am honored, Major," returned Deo Daley, his lips bent in a queer, sad smile. "But I must decline. I am not an army man—I am a trail scout. My duties are in demand, sir. Tomorrow I lead Tex Garland and Irene out of Fort Adios on a new quest of Terror Trail."

Disappointment glinted briefly in Major Fletcher's keen eyes. Then his lips softened in a smile.

"You are aware of the Army's new regulations regarding travel of wagon trains along Terror Trail?" he inquired. "That all such caravans must be accompanied by a representative of the Army—in the interest of combatting the Indian peril?"

Daley nodded, his eyes breaking attention a second time as they sought out Lieutenant Curt Thode among the guard of honor.

With your permission, Sir," the scout of Terror Trail said, "Lieutenant 'Thode will accompany us, as the Army's official representative. You see—uh—he has more of a personal interest in our—uh—expedition than anyone else under your command—"

Major Fletcher executed an about-face and returned Curt Thode's perfunctory salute from the ranks.

"You heard Daley's proposition, Lieutenant?" he asked. "Do you want to be placed on detached service long enough to see Mr. Garland's wagon train through to its destination?"

Curt Thode's black eyes glinted, but no man present had a true understanding of the thoughts which stormed behind those slitted orbs.

"Yes, sir," he replied. "I would enjoy such a break from the routine of the post, sir. Daley and I discussed the matter thoroughly before he suggested my appointment, sir."

Major Fletcher chewed his lower lip thoughtfully. He was recalling how, only a few short hours before, Lieutenant Thode had insisted that Deo Daley might try to desert, if granted his freedom. And now—

Shrugging off an unspoken thought, the commandant

of Fort Adios turned back to the scout before him.

"Very well," he said. "Lieutenant Thode shall accompany you, Daley, and will report back here for active duty at the completion of his mission with you. I wish you Godspeed through the Indian country."

TREASURE CASTLE

DAY HAD FOLLOWED DAY, until the scout of Terror Trail knew they must be near their destination. He glanced about him. An underground river had led them into a deep cylinder-shaped sink in the tangled mountains. Weather-bluffed cliff walls rose in silent majesty on all sides, surmounted by a sky of deepest blue.

Trees grew at the base of the cliffs. Generations of trees had grown and seeded and died, without white man's eyes being the wiser.

Daley gained the crest of the grassy little knoll, suddenly halted stock-still, eyes widened by the astonishing spectacle that met him.

The floor of the hollow was a green saucer, through which the Rio Torcido threaded like a rill of mercury. The hollow was three hundred yards across, as if a giant drill had bored out a hole in the mountains.

And in the center of that saucer, unreal as a mirage in the shadow of the rimming cliffs, stood a castle—a castle out of a story book.

A castle with gray moss-hung walls. A castle with battlements along its frowning ramparts, with loopholed turrets guarding its corners. Weird as a cemetery, and twice as foreboding.

A round tower of masonry lifted from the center of

that huge monument of ancient stone. A tower surmounted by a parapet with battlements, and rags of what had once been a pirate's black flag fluttering from a time-warped flagpole, stark against the sky.

The frowning walls were girdled by a stagnant moat with water pads forming a sour crust around the edges. A rotted and grass-grown drawbridge hung by rusty red chains in front of a bleak and gloomy gate in the wall— a gate that seemed to beckon the wide-eyed adventurers to the perils and mysteries which that ancient fortress contained.

"Irene! We've found it!"

Deo Daley's throat muscles worked, but no further sound came. It was not necessary. For they all knew now that they had reached their goal. They were face to face with the age-lost Spanish castle where a dashing pirate of days gone by had stored his ill-gotten loot of gold and jewels.

The *Alcazar de los Ladrones*—Castle of Thieves!

The castle was built of gray granite blocks, dotted with slotlike windows, cornered by cone-roofed turrets, and topped by a notched, overhanging battlement.

The time-scoured spire of a round tower lifted above the center of the Castle of Thieves, on top of which an ancient flagstaff still held aloft the rotted and flapping remnants of a sinister black banner.

A majestic castle it had once been, glamorous as old Spain. Now it was moss-grown, its stagnant moat fringed with sour scum, its drawbridge tufted with sprouting grass and supported by rust-red chains. Its stone walls were beginning to crumble with age.

"We're forgettin' that we've caught glimpses of what looked like Don Chirlo following us on the trail," said Deo Daley, turning to the men. "He's liable to follow us in here, so before we go to look the castle over, I suggest we leave a guard here at the mouth o' the cave."

Curt Thode rummaged in a hip pocket of his uniform to produce a dollar. He flipped it and clapped it to the back of his other hand.

"Call it, Garland!" invited Thode. "Heads? You're wrong—it's tails. That means it's between me an' you, Daley, to see who will guard the mouth o' this tunnel. Although I doubt if Don Chirlo would risk coming through there, anyway, in daytime."

Again the coin twinkled in the air, and the young scout called "heads" also. The Army man lifted his hand from the dollar, exposed the tails again, and shook his head.

"You're eliminated, too. There's no use o' me drawin'," said the cavalry officer, pocketing the coin. "Lead 'em to the castle, Daley. I'll stand guard over the cave. If you hear a shot, come a-runnin'—it'll mean Chirlo's comin'!"

Daley turned to the two Garlands, and grinned. "We better go while it's still light," he suggested, glancing toward the castle, which occupied the center of a grass-covered saucer at the base of the cliffs. "I'll relieve you pronto, Thode."

The scout of Terror Trail paused long enough to remove saddle and bridle from his coal-black cayuse, Gunpowder, that grazed nearby. No matter how pressing his business, Deo Daley never neglected his magnificent mount.

Curt Thode's mustached upper lip lifted in a leering grin, as he saw his three companions make their way across the meadowlike flat toward the *Alcazar de los Ladrones.*

The Army man's sweaty palm still clutched the coin

in his pocket, and he drew it forth, turning it over slowly between his fingers. Then he opened his other palm, to expose a second dollar.

One of the coins which Thode held in his hands was double-headed. The one he had flipped was double-tailed. More than once, his sleight-of-hand work with those coins had served Curt Thode well.

"Pretty neat, leavin' me for guard!" chuckled the spy of Don Chirlo's gang of crooks. "Pretty good—for Don Chirlo!"

Thode squatted on the heels of his amber-colored Army boots and chuckled to himself as he saw Deo Daley lead the two Garlands toward the Spanish castle which bulked like a gravestone in the bottom of the craterlike pit.

And indeed, each granite block in that fortress was the tombstone of some Apache slave whom Don Picadero had forced to be a mason, with no pay except death by club and fist and sword.

Watching, he saw Deo Daley and his two partners reach the moldy drawbridge at the entrance of the Castle of Thieves. The immensity of the structure only then became apparent to Thode. The three human beings were reduced to antlike proportions as they trod carefully out over the rotten and weed-grown bridge which spanned a foul, mosquito-swarming moat of mucky brown water.

Muscles tensed in Thode's body as he saw the trio pause in awe under the frowning walls of the ancient castle. The great iron-bolted pine gates of the Alcazar were opened on their rust-gnawed hinges. With a sigh of relief, Curt 'Mode saw Deo Daley and his friends make their way inside.

"You better enjoy yourself in there while you can!"

snarled the treacherous Army man, waving an imaginary farewell at the trio who had just disappeared inside the *Alcazar de los Ladrones*. " 'Cause you ain't ever goin' to carry out the gold you'll find in there. Not if my scheme works out!"

So saying, the cavalry rider laid his rifle next to Gunpowder's saddle, removed boots and spurs, unbuckled his gun belt and hung it on a cottonwood scrub, and made his way toward the bank of the whispery river which slid into the hole in the cliff.

Wriggling his bare toes to get a firm footing on a granite rimrock overlooking the eddying pool just outside the cavern mouth, Thode paused to take a last-minute check-up of his plans.

"While Daley's gloatin' about findin' the castle, an' leavin' Don Chirlo behind this way," reasoned Thode to himself, "he's plumb forgettin' that he'll be needin' grub—an' Don Chirlo has supplies an' pack burros."

Thode grinned to himself as he peered into the black depths of the tunnel, and prepared himself for his dive into the river.

"So the thing for me to do is to get in good with Chirlo again," decided the spy, plastering back his lacquer-black hair with both palms, "because even if Daley has grub, Don Chirlo's got us bottled up in here. Right now, Chirlo's sore at me for puttin' Daley out of the way, but I reckon he'll change his tune when I get through talkin' to 'im. "

Sucking in a deep breath, Curt Thode raised his arms and dived into the river.

Splash! The man's diving body cleft the water with a creamy surge.

His swimming strokes carried him deep into the pool, out into the current of the river. Then he was inside the tunnel which led through the cliff wall and out into the Gorge of La Crescenta Canyon, where Don Chirlo and his band had been blocked in their attempt to slay or capture Daley's party.

When Thode had come to the surface, he was far inside the tunnel. With hard strokes, he avoided crashing into submerged rocks. Daylight thinned as the swift current swept him to the crest of a foamy stair of rapids.

Spray plastered his hair. Water tore at his legs. Spume pounded his back like pebbles, as he sluiced his way through a roiling surge and then rolled like a soused rat into a stretch of quiet water at the base of the rapids.

Like a blackfish, Thode fought on into deepening water. The Rio Torcido slid him across gravel bars and around bends in the tunnel.

Then a half-moon of dazzling daylight smote Thode in the face, and he lodged against a foamy cleaver of rock, where he lay, gasping, his buckshot eyes blinking in the light.

Out there, gathered on the bank of the Rio Torcido, about twenty outlaws were standing, gesturing, arguing.

Heart pounding, Curt Thode dived once more into the current, and before he had come to the surface again he saw the black water go green and then blinding white, and he was outside the tunnel and swimming through a milling pool on the very bank of which Chirlo's crooks had assembled.

"Hola!" came a throaty Mexican voice. "It's Thode!"

Thode knifed his way through the millrace of water to a bank whippy with willow growth, and climbed out on the ground. He paled as he got to his feet, dripping, to stare into twenty leveled six-guns and rifles. Would he be shot down?

"So you came back to Don Chirlo to keel you, no?" barked the outlaw in a voice like a saw cutting raw bones. He clamped a viselike hand on Thode's wet shoulder and gouged the muzzle of a silver-mounted .45 in the spy's ribs.

Trembling with horror, Curt Thode backed away, Chirlo following him, the pressure of the hand on his shoulder making the Army man wince with pain.

"We—we have them trapped, Chirlo!" gasped the spy. "All the time, I been serving you. Watching and waitin' my chance! Now I come out here—to tell you about the Castle of Thieves. Ah—now you listen!"

The outlaws gathered about the trembling spy as they heard him unfold the amazing story of the treasure castle which lay on the opposite side of the great cliff.

When the spy finished speaking, Don Chirlo's scar-scribbled face lost some of its fierceness, and he released Thode to jam his silver six-gun into its holster. Grinning like a well-fed panther, the big outlaw chief turned slowly to his gang.

"We apologize to *Señor* Thode, no?" he laughed, speaking in Spanish. "Come, *amigos*—to your horses! We will follow *Señor* Thode to the Alcazar!"

Gun barrels glinted in the sunlight and hoofs splashed sheets of water as the entire band of crooks, who a few moments before had thought themselves blocked at the very threshold of victory, plunged their jaded saddle horses into the laundry-suds chute which spilled out of the Rio Torcido's cavern.

INTO THE CASTLE

A PIECE OF ICE seemed to slide down Deo Daley's spine as he set foot on the rotten, pulpy logs which formed the drawbridge spanning the moat of the *Alcazar de los Ladrones*.

"We'll be lucky if this damned thing doesn't bust!" grunted the young scout, as the three picked their way cautiously over the bridge. "Those chains don't look any too strong, either, after three hundred years o' weatherin' "

A twenty-foot hem of shelving dirt, covered with a rug of tangled blue-stem grass, thistle poppies, and ignota brush, lay between the inner edge of the ditch and the base of the castle walls.

The huge proportions of the castle took their breath away as they stared up at the beetling, age-blasted face of the wall. The sun was setting over the Rocky Mountain peaks outside, and the loopholed turrets on each corner of the wall were edged in scarlet.

"There'll be only another hour or so o' daylight, down in the bottom o' this hole!" ventured old Tex Garland, rummaging into his buckskins and drawing out his smelly corncob pipe, which he crowded with tobacco and jabbed between his teeth. "So we better get looking while there's still light enough to go by, huh?"

Like little children approaching a dark room, the three adventurers crept closer to the quarter-opened gates of the Castle of Thieves. Time had opened those iron-bolted pine-log gates, and the hinges had rusted tightly, holding them ajar.

Deo Daley loosened his six-gun in its holster. Then,

taking Irene by the hand, he stole through the narrow opening and stood at last—inside the ancient castle of Don Picadero!

In awed silence, the three halted there and gaped in amazement at the scene which met their gaze. It was a sight such as no man's eyes had ever before witnessed— a devil's stage, set with the rotted husks of human beings for actors.

The four walls of the castle fenced in a plaza or courtyard, which was dotted here and there by sprawling, armor-clad skeletons—bodies of the Spanish pirates who had been starved to death by besieging Indians of long ago, who were in turn avenging the murders of their brothers who had been slain after the castle was built.

Grass grew deep in the courtyard. Vines crawled up the damp, rotten walls. Bones of centuries-dead horses had been consumed by the buzzards who had wheeled down out of the stern, brassy sky, with rending beaks and tearing talons.

The castle itself was in the center of the square, nearly filling it. Like a box set inside another box, so that the courtyard was a masonry-walled canyon, as dark as the inside of an opened coffin, weighted with silence and must and stagnant air.

A flight of steps led into an arched doorway before them. With quaking hearts and pale faces, the three gold seekers made their way toward the door in stunned silence, creeping as if fearful of awakening the yellow skeletons that slept about them.

"I—I wish we'd waited until daylight!" declared Irene with a nervous laugh as they mounted the moss-grown steps. "It's like digging into a grave."

A wooden door had once barred the opening, but it had long since been battered to splinters by raging winds sucking down inside the castle walls. Through it they went, into a damp, sour-smelling hallway lined with doors and dimly lighted through slitted paneless windows in the castle walls overhead.

Uncanny! Their footsteps started hollow echoes to gossiping inside the murky corridor as they stole down its length. Echoes which seemed to mutter about the ghostly footsteps of the Spanish criminals who had died in this tomblike storehouse of ill-gotten treasure, long ages before.

In a shadowy stretch of the hallway, Tex Garland, puffing blue clouds of tobaccoo smoke through his ragged brush of beard, suddenly tripped over a prone object which rattled like tin pots and pans. He leaped to his feet, then scissored out an oath as he saw that he had stumbled on another skeleton in armor.

A grinning, greenish-hued skull leered up out of a corroded steel helmet. One bony hand still clutched a Toledo blade.

It reminded Deo Daley of the similar skeleton which Curt Thode and he had found in that cave out on Destruction Desert—the skeleton that had yielded the secret map which had begun this amazing adventure.

"Come on—here's a flight of stairs!" whispered the scout of Terror Trail, his voice sounding weird and ghostly as it was caught up and repeated in a thousand shadowy niches and doorways. "The treasure must be in one o' these rooms!"

Up the dust-carpeted stairs they went, cringing away from a twisted skeleton in moldy rags which had evidently been carrying a jar of water to the Spanish warriors on the castle roof, when death had struck.

Slick with sweat, grinning sheepishly at each other in the stilly darkness, the trio gained a landing and stood

64

for a moment regaining their breath, though the climb had not been a severe one.

"Here's a curtain—let's mosey through there!" suggested Tex Garland, curling gnarled fingers over the butt of his Colt .45.

A thick-walled doorway was at their right. Deo Daley reached out, his hand recoiling as he touched the damp, soggy hangings. They felt cold and repulsive, like a dead snake's scales.

A ragged rent dropped out of the curtain cloth as Daley shoved the heavy, green-molded folds aside. Hand on gun butt—the feel of his six-gun seemed to quiet the scout's jumpy nerves—Deo Daly led the two through the opening, and into a great flagstone-paved room nearly eighty feet square.

It was evidently the main lobby, or banquet hall, of the Castle of Thieves. Its floor was a checkerboard of basalt and granite, roughly hewn and thickly layered with the dust of forgotten ages.

Light streamed down in bars from slotlike windows above, to reveal massive wooden furniture on the lobby floor, and a balcony skirting all four walls of the room and reached by a grand staircase across the floor from where the three wide-eyed people stood.

A gigantic fireplace, blackened by the soot of long - ago fires, occupied a fourth of one wall. The walls were hung with ancient battle-axes and shields, spears and swords, attesting to the fights which Don Picadero and his pirates had won.

Each weapon, no doubt, was a grim trophy of a battle waged back in the dim beginnings of American history. Each shield, battered by blade and lance, could tell its chill story of death and high adventure.

This lobby, at least, seemed empty of skeletons. But

65

the air was dank with the fusty odor of corpses long since crumbled into dust. The visitors' very breathing was magnified into the awful wheezing of some great monster's dragonlike lungs.

Deo Daley turned to his two companions, his bronzed face taking on a sickly hue in the greenish light which filtered down through the window slits behind the balcony.

"Did you ever see such a ghostly place?" He shivered, craning his neck to peer upward at the heavy stone-railed balcony which rimmed the room. "Almost expect a gory pile o' bones to come chasin' out o' the shadows to grab you, huh?"

Irene's lips parted in a weak smile. Her nerves were steadier, now that she had left those moldy, armored bones behind, downstairs.

"Doesn't that grand stairway look majestic?" she said, leading the way out into the center of the echoing room. "Just like I used to read about in fairy tales. Can't you almost imagine an elfin queen descending those steps with her trailing silken train?"

Deo Daly's spurs chimed in the ghostly silence as he followed her toward the foot of the staircase. Tex Garland was close behind, puffing his corncob like a laboring engine.

"No women were ever inside o' Don Chirlo's Castle o' Thieves, Irene," he replied, smiling. "I reckon you're the first girl who ever graced this pirate banquet hall with her presence."

A quarter of the way up the stair steps, the three suddenly came to a halt, eyes glued to the head of the flight above them.

A ladder of golden sunset glow was streaming through a window far above and behind them, falling through the intervening space like a shaft of yellow fire, to land in a blazing rectangle upon the wall at the head of the stairs. And centered in that amazing spotlight was a great oil painting in a gilded frame of tremendous proportions.

"I've heard o' that picture!" exclaimed Deo Daley breathlessly. "It's a portrait o' Don Picadero himself. The Injuns talk about it in their legends o' the Alcazar. They thought it was haunted—bein' the first paintin' they'd ever seen in those days. Picadero was a vain hombre, an' he brought it here to set up."

It was an uncanny painting. It must have been the work of some Old World master. Towering eight feet high and six feet wide, it depicted in lifesize proportions a slender Spanish caballero and his white steed, standing in the background.

So expert was the artistry of brush and pigment that the scaled and time-rotted canvas still held a lifelike quality which made the three spectators feel as if they were actually gazing upon the ancient Spanish pirate in person.

Don Picadero was tall, clad in white satin vest and trousers now faded and stained by time. The pirate's waist was girdled by a purple silk sash, and one hand held a golden-hilted sword.

The buccaneer's face was a pasty blob ornamented with a curling brace of spike-tipped reddish-brown mustaches. The features were over-shadowed by a wide-brimmed hat heavily plumed with ostrich feathers that had once been blue.

In the background of the painting, almost invisible in the canvas, the artist had painted Don Picadero's famous white steed, White Cloud—a horse which Indian legendry said was winged, and protected Don

Picadero from arrow or battle-ax when he was mounted on it.

"Too bad Don Picadero's life couldn't have been saved by his white horse while the 'Paches were besiegin' this castle, but White Cloud wasn't proof against starvation," laughed Daley, after he had explained the fable of the Spanish pirate's steed to the two Garlands. "Somewhere inside of these very walls, we'll find the bones of old Don Picadero himself, as well as his gold."

"DEATH FOR DALEY!"

HORSES SPLASHED and snorted as the bandit gang of Don Chirlo emerged from the mouth of the Rio Torcido, to battle the sluggish current as they fought their way out on a sand pit and shook water from their coats. Up on the knoll, Deo Daley's beautiful black, Gunpowder, whickered an innocent greeting.

"An' there's the famous lost Castle o' Thieves, *amigos!*" called Thode in a low voice, as the killer crew assembled at the top of the grassy knoll. "Everybody better talk low—we don't want the scout o' Terror Trail to hear us!"

For many minutes, the case-hardened outlaws of Don Chirlo's band stood in awed silence, as they gazed upon the granite walls and slotted turrets of the *Alcazar de los Ladrones*.

"What a place for a hide-out for our own gang!" jabbered Don Chirlo, his eyes pin points of greed. "*Caramba*, what a place!"

The sun was setting in a lake of scarlet behind the Rockies, filling the craterlike hole with gauzy haze.

The pointed spires of the lost castle were rimmed with blazing light, and the ancient rags of the pirate flag on the warped pole fluttered lazily.

"All we have to do now," decided Don Chirlo in Spanish, "is to kill Daley, the old man, and the girl. Hah, *compadres,* tonight we shall dine in the banquet hall of Don Picadero!"

Dismounting and leaving their jaded horses to graze beside Gunpowder—the animals were too exhausted from their week's trek across Destruction Desert to require a guard—the file of men headed across the grassy bottom of the pocket.

The Rio Torcido wound like a platinum belt through the saucer-shaped greensward. Don Picadero had indeed chosen well the place to hide his gold and build his Spanish castle.

The pine-hung rimrocks above could not be reached on foot. A sky view of the lost Alcazar was available only to the cruising hawks and buzzards.

There was grass and water enough in this pothole to last an Army's remuda for months. In fact, the legends of the Apaches who had starved out Picadero's band recorded that it had taken six moons to kill the last of the pirates inside the Alcazar walls.

At a signal from Curt Thode, the band became silent, as they approached the decayed drawbridge. A whispered conference at the edge of the stale, grass-bordered moat led them to decide to cross the shaky bridge one by one, rather than trust the ancient span with their combined weight. The waiting outlaws took advantage of the pause to reload their six-guns and rifles with fresh shells.

Five minutes later, the entire band was clustered by the iron-bolted pine gates which Deo Daley and his comrades had entered, a quarter hour before them.

The beady-eyed Apache warriors in the band were waxy with sweat. Their old Indian forefathers had deemed this place a haunt of evil spirits, and only their cruel and savage pride instilled enough courage in them to remain with Chirlo's band, here at the very threshold of the Castle of Thieves.

One by one, the outlaws crept through the gateway and out into the courtyard. The dying sun rays shed sparks off unsheathed guns. Every face was grimy with sweat; every hand clutched a knife or six-gun or Winchester.

Moving stealthily, guided toward the castle proper by the towering bulk of their leader, Chirlo, the fiendish but quaking horde of men made their way, heads darting about, eyes alert for a glimpse of the scout of Terror Trail or one of his party.

Boot soles grated on the castle steps as Don Chirlo led his trembling men into the murky depths of the castle hallway. At his side paced Curt Thode, the spy, his treacherous heart pumping against his ribs, his thumb holding a .45 six-gun at full cock.

Don Chirlo held out a hand as they finished climbing the first set of stairs, at the end of the hallway. His mahogany-hued face worked in the gloom. Flashing eyes and snarling teeth glittered in the ghostly light. Curt Thode shuddered. He knew that every man in the gang felt like bolting from this weird place.

"Keep behind this curtain here!" whispered Don Chirlo, pointing to the rotted drapes through which Deo Daley and his party had gone. "You'll hide here. Thode and I'll go on ahead. When you hear me whistle, come quickly!"

With the panicky outlaws remaining behind, Don

70

Chirlo and Curt Thode made their way through the curtain and out to the edge of the banquet-hall floor. With gun out and lips drawn tight over grated teeth, Curt Thode obeyed orders and went ahead, in search of Deo Daly and Tex Garland and the beautiful Irene.

"Irene turned me down for that tramp Daley, back at Fort Adios!" grated the traitor bitterly. "Now she'll be sorry—when I'm tossin' her into that stinkin' moat outside, to go down gurglin', bound hand an' foot!"

Slithering along through the shadows a few feet behind the cavalryman came the black, silver-ornamented figure of Don Chirlo, alert to back Thode's play in case the Daley party became suspicious, when they saw Thode approaching.

Long had Chirlo awaited this moment—the moment when he could slay with his own hands the daring young scout of Terror Trail. In Chirlo's merciless brain burned one flaming purpose: Death for Daley!

***

Deo Daley noticed that on either side of the life-sized portrait of Don Picadero, there was a coffin-shaped doorway. As they reached the level of the balcony floor, the scout left his two companions standing in mute awe before the painting of the ancient buccaneer, and peered cautiously through the left-hand of the two doors.

"Hm-m-m," mused the scout of Terror Trail, turning to regard his two friends. "This is the foot of the big central tower we saw from outside, I reckon."

Coming forward, the two Garlands stepped through the doorway behind Daley, to find themselves in a circular chamber, up which wound a spiral stairway, as in a lighthouse tower.

Far above them, through the center of the corkscrew of stone steps, they could see daylight—the top of the lookout pinnacle.

"I think I'll take a run up there for a look-see at how Curt Thode's gettin' along guardin' the cave," decided Deo Daley, adjusting the brim of his scratch-finish Stetson. "We've been gone almost a half hour now, an' if Don Chirlo's devils try to storm us through that underground river, he might be needin' help. I can see him from the top o' the tower, easily."

At the foot of the stairwell Daley turned, a smile lighting his handsome, wind-bronzed features. He shook his head as Irene stepped forward, followed by her grizzled father.

"No use o' you two wearin' yourselves out climbin' those steps," advised the scout of Terror Trail, patting the girl's shoulder. "You stay here with Tex. You might look around an' try to spot a good dry room where we can sleep tonight. Those Spaniards must have had bedrooms."

Irene toyed with the necklace of bear's claws which adorned her neck. She was a genuine prairie beauty, in her doeskin blouse which glittered in the subdued light from the wealth of Indian beadwork which decorated it. Beneath the folds of her split-type buckskin skirt the toes of brown riding boots peeped. She wore a six-gun and bowie knife belted to her waist.

"All right, Deo, but hurry back!" replied the girl anxiously, as old Tex Garland rubbed a whiskery cheek against hers and put a fringed sleeve around her waist. "Something tells me it would be better to stick together."

With a laugh intended to quiet the girl's forebodings, Deo Daley started lightly up the winding steps. But in his own heart still clung that peculiar uneasiness which he had first felt, even as he entered this unlucky castle of doom.

"I must be gettin' nervous in my old age!" grunted the scout to himself as he slogged on up the twisting steps. "Thode said he'd fire a shot if he heard or saw anything suspicious. An' once dark comes, there isn't much danger o' those skunks o' Don Chirlo's riskin' wadin' through that underground river, I reckon."

About forty feet up the tower, Daley paused to swab sweat off his Stetson band. A tiny loophole pierced the four-foot thickness of the tower walls, and he peered through a screen of gray cobwebs to obtain a view of the slate-roofed castle top, with the pine-furred crest of the opposite rim of the pipelike pit in which the Alcazar was built, forming the background.

"I can't let Tex or Irene know I'm worried," the young plainsman muttered as he resumed climbing, "but after we locate the gold in this castle, what then? Don Chirlo can keep guard out there in La Crescenta Canyon an' starve us out. I'm hungry enough to chew on a stewed hoof right now!"

Another forty, muscle-grinding feet Daley climbed, while sweat bubbled from his pores, and his breath wheezed through dry lips. This stairway was little more than a ladder and had been but roughly hewn from granite blocks, so that the soles of his moccasin clad feet were beginning to throb from the strain.

He found still another loophole, through which an eerie wind moaned, making ice-drops out of the sweat on his neck as he paused there and sponged off his face with a bandanna.

In the ghostly light which filtered through the spider meshes of the loophole, Daley caught sight of a crumpled junk-pile of rusty tin and chain mail, through which yellowed bones peeped, and several feet to one side a rat-chewed skull with hair clinging to its parchment scalp like a hank of thread regarded him with a toothy grin.

"Ugh!" shuddered Daley, climbing another couple of turns to get the grim picture out of view. "Died with an arrow in his head, probably—some 'Pache sharpshooter got 'im when he was stickin' his head through the loophole."

The tower was getting lighter, and as he looked up through the beads of perspiration which clung to his eyelashes, the young scout of Terror Trail heaved a sigh of relief as he saw that only a half dozen more turns of the stairs would deposit him on the circular platform which roofed the lookout spire.

Meanwhile, down on the balcony overlooking Don Picadero's banquet hall, Irene Garland and her father were strolling about, peering into curtain-shrouded doorways, inspecting racked armor and rust-speckled lances and swords.

"Just think, Daddy—any door we might open might be the one to Don Picadero's treasure chamber!" exclaimed Irene, her eyes like twin blue stars. "Isn't it thrilling?"

The old buckskin-clad pioneer stoked his corncob with tobacco and lighted up as they resumed their march around the balcony.

"It'd be a damned sight more thrillin' to me to find the kitchen larder, I'm thinkin'!" grunted the practical old frontiersman, dribbling smoke ribbons through a screen of salt-grey beard. "My stomach's buttoned to my backbone now, an' no gold coins or jewelry would satisfy the rats that's gnawin' at my vitals right this min—"

Garland broke off. The two spun about, startled, as, a

jingle of spur chains and the sound of high-heeled boots reached their ears. Someone was striding rapidly across the floor below.

Tex rushed to the stone railing of the balcony, gun drawn, eyes peering down on the broad, smooth floor of Don Picadero's banqueting lobby. A sneer curled his lips as he turned.

"Huh! I thought so!" he snorted, jabbing his gun in its holster and heading for the stairway. "It's Thode. We left him to guard entrance to this crater hole, an' he's gone an' left his post, he's so damned curious to get into this Castle o' Thieves an' help hunt the gold!"

With Irene at his side, Tex Garland stalked to the head of the stairs. As they stood there looking down, father and daughter saw the erect figure of Curt Thode climbing the stairs, three steps at a time, to meet them.

"Thode! What in hell are you doin' in here without a man to relieve you on guard?" demanded Garland, as the Army man came to a stop on the step just under the old pioneer's booted feet. "Them skunks o' Don Chirlo's might try to rush us."

"Close-hobble your trap an' tell me where Daley is!" interrupted Thode, with a surly scowl.

"Deo's up in the tower," Irene put in, "looking for you.

A savage leer twisted Thode's lips off his gums. Hooking one hand in his gun belt, he knotted the right fist into a rock-hard ball of knuckles. Without warning, the big traitor brought up his arm in a whizzing uppercut.

Ordinarily, the punch would have split a man's jawbone, but Tex Garland's chin was padded with a tough mattress of wiry bristles. The blow landed soddenly, and the old man staggered back. Then he fell,

75

the back of his head cracking hard on the stone floor of the balcony as he stretched his length and lay there limply.

The painting of Don Picadero looked down at the body sprawled with outflung arms below, and seemed to smile.

"Curt! What in heaven's name are you—"

Anger cut off the girl's gasp of astonishment, and then her hand blurred to her side, and she whipped out a blue-barreled Colt.

In two catlike steps, Thode was before her, as the gun muzzle swung up and covered his midriff, held as steady as a rock.

"Don't touch me, Thode! You had no call to hit my dad like that when he wasn't expec—"

Slap! Clang! Thode's palm flew out and knocked the gun from the girl's grasp and sent it bouncing metallically down the steps.

Words boiled hotly through the spy's teeth as the girl twisted back, away from his clutching fingers.

"Your ol' man's been rowelin' me long enough, savvy? From now on I'm ramroddin' this—"

With a gasp of terror, the girl fled before the murder-light which gleamed in Curt Thode's eyes. Darting aside like a rabbit, she sprang to the head of the stairs and was racing down the stone steps like a deer, Thode sprinting at her heels.

There was no time to scoop up her gun, lodged on a step. But across the banquet hall hung a rack of swords, and if she could get one of them in her grasp she knew she could defend herself against a dozen of Curt Thode's stripe.

But even as she reached the floor of the banquet hall, a black-clad figure suddenly darted like a hairy spider out of a blot of shadow under the balustrade.

Light gleamed dully on fanglike teeth and silver spangles which decorated a black-velvet jacket and bell-bottomed Spanish trousers.

"Deo! Deeeo! He-e-e-elp!"

The girl's pealing, high-pitched scream shattered the stillness, as Don Chirlo's great arms snapped out to sweep her off her feet. Struggling futilely against a bearlike hug, the girl felt strangling thumbs sink in her throat.

Darkness engulfed her as Don Chirlo's snarl of triumph smote her eardrums. The outlaw chief hurled her limp body roughly to the floor and looked up, to grin at the advancing Curt Thode.

ON THE TOWER TOP

DEO DALEY, panting like a landed trout as he gained the topmost step of the circular stairway which climbed the Alcazar's central and highest tower, took off his Stetson and let the cool breath of the dusk fan his beaded face.

He was standing on a round balcony, twenty feet in diameter, which formed the roof of the lookout pinnacle. Just before him, in the center of the floor, rose the splintery, crack-seamed shaft of the flagpole, at the top of which still fluttered the pitch-soaked cloth of Don Picadero's black flag.

"Whew! I'd hate to scale this tower at sunrise an' sunset every day, to put out those colors!" gasped the scout of Terror Trail, replacing his sombrero after combing moisture out of his brown, wavy hair with spread fingers. "It's tough to work up an appetite when you don't know where your next meal is—"

Daley's mouth suddenly snapped shut, tongue gluing to the roof of his mouth. For as his eyes swept over the roof floor, they fastened upon the stretched-out body of a mummylike corpse, lying at the base of the flagstaff before him!

An ancient rawhide halyard extended from the body and up the flagpole—the rope that had drawn that pirate flag to the peak of the staff, generations before!

The body was pithy-dry, having lain out here on the roof of this amazing castle tower, exposed to the blazing suns and dry, curing air of the centuries.

Stealing forward, Deo Daley knelt beside the body, reached out a timid hand, and touched the rich snowy cloth which formed the jacket of the mummy. Gleaming white satin, trimmed with a hem of green-tarnished but genuine gold brocade.

A purple silk sash girdled the body's waist. A gold-hilted sword hung in a rusty scabbard beside white-trousered legs. Jammed on the skeleton's head was a wide-brimmed hat with a wispy sweep of ostrich plumage that had once been bright blue.

In Deo's mind's eye, there grew a vividly distinct memory: the painting of the white-clad, plume-hatted Spanish gentleman of that faded and peeling oil portrait, down at the head of the castle's lobby stairway.

"Don Picadero!" The words burst from Daley's lips.

Too overawed even to breathe, the scout of Terror Trail pressed aside the crackling, time-stiffened brim of the mummy's hat, and peered down upon a leathery, shrunken face as twisted and wrinkled as a puckered fig.

The resemblance was unmistakable. There were the withered eyelids couched in blotter-dry sockets of the skull. A nose like a falcon's beak, nostrils sewn together by the drying action of New Mexico's baking suns and searing winds blasting over the roof of the tower.

Reddish-brown mustaches with spiked tips, sprouting from an upper lip as wooden as a mummy's.

New sweat started from Deo Daley's face as he stood up, shivering suddenly in the evening breeze which sighed through the square-notched battlements of the ancient observation tower.

"Deo! Deeeo! He-e-e-elp!"

As unreal as the cry of a far-off coyote baying at the moon, came the faint treble of a woman's voice, spiraling up through the tower beneath him to reach Deo Daley's ears.

The scout spun about, eyes wide, mouth screwed into a tense line. Had he imagined seeing those horses, hearing that cry?

But no! Startled birds were winging away from their nests in the crannies of the turret eaves below, voicing scared cries, as the echoes floated back from the cliffs:

"Deo! Deeeo! He-e-e-lp!"

Springing over the crusty body of Don Picadero, Deo Daley's moccasined feet pattered across the tower roof and in a trice he had ducked into the dark throat of the tower stairway.

Fleet as a mountain goat, swift as a descending panther, the scout of Terror Trail whirled down the corkscrew stairs, gun in hand, veins frozen strings of ice in his body.

With the wind whistling by his ears, Deo Daley bounded to the circular room in the bottom of the tower and shot through the coffin-shaped doorway beside the painting of Don Picadero.

He slid to a stop on the smooth stone floor of the balcony, and his heart jelled as he teetered over the inert form of old Tex Garland, head lolling beside a corncob pipe which still trickled smoke threads.

"Tex! Tex! What's hap—"

A sound cranked Daley's head about on his shoulders, and his face went hot and a look that was not pleasant to see kindled in his eyes as he spotted the form of Curt Thode standing at the base of the stairs, a taunting grin on his face, his arms folded. No trace of Irene Garland did the scout see.

"Thode, damn you! You've left the place unguarded, an' they must o' come in. I saw horses—"

Down the steps at a bounding stride went Deo Daley, eyes blazing rage, brown hand clutching the red butt of his .45. Thode was rocking on the balls of his feet, a smirking leer on his Swarthy, narrow face.

"Where in hell is Irene?" yelled the scout, jabbing his gun muzzle in Thode's stomach. "What happened to the old man?"

Still Curt Thode made no reply, his smirk widening. "Answer me, damn you!" yelled the scout in a louder voice, his finger tightening on the trigger. "I heard Irene yell, an' now she's gone! I tell you, I think Don Chirlo's got in—an' you sit there an grin! Answer me, you hear, or I'll send a slug through your lousy yellow-striped bel—"

Thode's button-black eyes slitted. He lifted an eyebrow, glanced beyond Daley's shoulder, and muttered a single sentence.

"Before you go shootin' anybody, Daley, look behind you!"

Not to be tricked, Daley stepped back, shoulders crouched, gun held steady on the cavalry officer. Then a sound of a cocking gun made the scout realize Thode's warning had not been a hoax. Still holding Thode under

80

the threat of his .45 six-gun, Daley turned his head to look.

Brrrang! The Castle of Thieves exploded with a crashing sound to accompany a stinging throb of agony as a bullet knocked the six-gun from Daley's grasp.

The weapon went skidding across the floor of Don Picadero's banquet floor.

"You're covered, *Señor* Daley! *Manos altos!*"

Ruby drops dribbled from the scout's bruised fingers, but that was not why his stomach went suddenly sick, as he felt his powers ebbing from his bones like flour from a ripped sack. Striding out of the shadows, his six-gun trailing a rope of weaving smoke, came the mahogany-faced form of Don Chirlo, most cruel of frontier outlaws. Doom had come at last . . .

Don Chirlo whistled, and the signal was answered instantly by a drumming of booted feet across the room.

Deo Daley's heart sank as he saw the forms of half-naked, leering Apaches emerge through the curtained entrance of the room, followed by whiskered and gun-freighted American crooks.

Two Indians came forward at a jerk of Chirlo's head, and Deo Daley found himself relieved of his bowie knife, frisked expertly for hidden weapons, and then seized on both sides by guards.

The young scout's face worked, eyes blazing wrathfully at the smirking Curt Thode, who strolled over to take his place beside the outlaw king, fingertips stroking his sideburns as he held one elbow in the palm of his opposite hand.

"This—so—this is your work, huh?" whispered the trail scout, his face going white as he began to realize the part Curt Thode had played. "Did you sell out just now to these skunks—or have you been a yellow traitor

81

all this time, wearin' Don Chirlo's collar an' ribbin' up this play?"

Don Chirlo came up, holstering his silver-mounted gun. He turned to Curt Thode and winked.

"*Señor* Thode has long been een my employ," stated the outlaw in groping English. "Tell heem your story, Thode. Tees scout of Terror Trail will be interes'."

And so while Deo Daley stood tense as a caged lion in the grasp of the two iron-muscled Apaches who held him from flying at Thode's throat, the young scout heard from beginning to end the appalling revelation of the Army man's treachery.

To conclude his recital, Thode stepped back in the shadows and produced Irene Garland, as limp as a dishrag, her skin the color of old chalk.

For an instant, the scout of Terror Trail thought the girl was already dead, until he caught a slight movement of breathing. Then his rage boiled over, and he writhed furiously between his guards.

"You dirty, crawlin' worm!" Deo Daley's torrent of rage was blocked by a stinging slap which brought threads of blood spurting from crushed lips, as Curt Thode stepped forward and planted a neck-snapping blow to the defenseless scout's face.

"Tie him up, men!" ordered the spy. "Tomorrow, Daley, you're goin' to be hung face downward from one o' the turrets, for the buzzards to play with. The gal an' her ol' man—they'll die, too, Daley, before we get Don Picadero's gold an' leave this place."

Something seemed to snap in Deo Daley's heart, and with a convulsive jerk he threw his guards aside and charged forward like a raging madman at the army officer.

Crash! Don Chirlo's gun barrel whished through the

air and thudded against Daley's skull.

The scout's knees buckled, the air went out of his lungs with a whistle, and he collapsed like a pole-axed beef.

Chirlo holstered the weapon and turned to issue a stern order.

"See to tying up thees hombre yourself, *Señor* Thode!" commanded the leader of the outlaws. "I weel take care of the others."

The lobby of the ancient castle rang with sound for the first time in centuries, as the outlaw band of Don Chirlo proceeded to dispose of their prisoners. Men went in groups of two and three through the entire castle, searching for Picadero's treasure coffers and at the same time hunting for a suitable place to imprison their captives until daylight should bring their torture.

Curt Thode, personally attending to the job of binding Deo Daley, was not satisfied until the scout of Terror Trail was trussed like a mummy, with heavy knotted ropes binding his wrists and elbows, knees and ankles.

An Apache brave dragged Irene Garland out on the floor and lashed her securely with a hemp rope.

Don Chirlo strode down the grand staircase, after pausing a moment to inspect the oil painting of Don Picadero, and bawled across the lobby to Curt Thode:

"I have found a prison, Thode! The top room of one of the corner turrets, on the outside wall. Bars on the windows!"

Don Chirlo paused long enough to issue orders to his men to take care of the horse which they had left outside. Others he sent to La Crescenta Canyon, to undertake the grueling task of getting the pack burros with the gang's food supplies safely through the underground river and into the pothole.

83

"I shall take for myself the *caballo* of *Señor* Daley," gloated the outlaw, rubbing his palms together with satisfaction as he mentally pictured the splendid animal which belonged to Deo Daley. "Gunpowder, he is called? Good! The finest horse in the world. Now he ees mine!"

With Apache guards carrying the still unconscious figures of Tex Garland and his daughter and the rope-wrapped, senseless figure of Deo Daley, Don Chirlo led his bandit gang through the curtained door of the banquet hall, down the flight of stairs to the long hallway, and thence to the outer portal of the Alcazar.

Across the grassy courtyard they went, groping in the dusk which pooled thickest here beneath the towering walls of the Alcazar *de los Ladrones*.

Don Chirlo skirted the base of the vine-plastered granite wall until he found a heavy hinged door in one corner. Entering, he led the outlaws up a twisting stairway which led into the turret above.

The group stopped as they reached the top floor of the cone-roofed turret. At a motion from Chirlo, Curt Thode stepped forward, found a heavy oaken door in the gloom, swung it open on its corroded hinges, and revealed a tiny cell lighted by a single window which was heavily grated with rusty bars.

" *'Sta bueno,* Chirlo!" complimented Thode, sizing up the dark room. "Our prisoners ain't goin' to git out o' this very easy!"

Hinges squealed as the ancient door was opened wider. The footsteps of the outlaws resounded in the tiny prison room. The single tiny window was so loaded with matted cobwebs as to permit only a slight wash of light. A flurry of bats flapped squeaking through a hole among the rafters of the tepee-shaped roof above.

Irene Garland was showing signs of returning to consciousness, so a second heavy lariat of manila hemp was produced by one of the gunmen and the girl was again tied, hands behind her back, and dumped into the prison cell.

Deo Daley was next to be dragged into the gloomy pit of the turret chamber. A raw welt on his scalp oozed blood to make a smeary track across the stones.

Tex Garland, groaning through his whiskers, was given another frisking to make sure his buckskins did not conceal any sheath knife or other weapon. Garland had also been trussed, with a braided rawhide reata.

Chirlo and Thode saw to it that the oak-slabbed door was tightly closed, and a sliding wooden bar jammed into place. As an extra precaution, they stationed a towering Mexican outlaw beside the turret door, armed with two six-guns and a knife.

Chuckling like a pair of hyenas returning from a successful kill, the half-breed outlaw king and his spy hurried down the turret steps together.

"Daley loves the *señorita,*" Thode was saying. "We will hang Daley by the heels over the parapet, where he can see us throw Irene into the moat to drown, with her hands tied behind her. The father shall see it too, before we tie him under a bucking horse's hoofs. and then we'll take Daley—"

"An' whack off hees *cabeza* weeth wan of the beeg swords I see hang een the banquet hall, *si!*" proposed the big outlaw leader. "Hees neck I shall cut off een two pieces."

DIVE OF DEATH

SOMETHING LIKE A HOT HAMMER seemed to pound
Deo Daley's scalp as the cold floor on which he lay
served to bring him back to his senses. Opening his
eyes, he found that night had fallen over the Castle of
Thieves, and that a thin bar of moonlight was coming
through the square of window.

For many minutes, the young plainsman writhed at
his bonds, while sweat seeped down off his scalp to
sting the sticky welt on his head like whisky in a raw
wound.

Moaning, the young scout of Terror Trail stopped
wrenching at the ropes, realizing that Chirlo's outlaws
had tied him up to stay.

"Deo! Deo!" Out of the gloom came a tense whisper,
and a warm stir of emotion went through the scout's
body as he recognized the hushed voice of Irene
Garland. "Awake, Deo?"

Daley licked his lips, pulled a breath into his lungs,
and answered: "Yeah. But I don't deserve to be, lettin'
Curt Thode pull the wool over my eyes like he did. Just
think—that crook betrayed Fort Adios an'—"

The girl's rope-wrapped body rolled over to his side.

"Ssh!" cautioned Irene, her lips to Daley's ear.
"There's a guard outside. We mustn't let him know
we're awake. I've just been waiting for you to regain
consciousness, Deo. I have a plan. It must be nearly
midnight, and we've got to escape before dawn. They—
they're planning all kinds of horrid torture for us." A
smile bent Daley's lips. "You're a thoroughbred, Irene,"
he breathed. "Here I am, crabbin' about Thode double-

crossin' us, when I ought be thinkin' o' some way to escape."

Irene Garland whispered again, her voice reviving the strength and courage in the scout's body, like some rare wine:

"But maybe—I think—I *have* figured out a way to get ourselves loose, anyway!" she answered. "That's why I've been waiting for you—to awaken. Daddy is still unconscious, but he's breathing better. He fell and hit the back of his head."

"What is your plan, Irene?" Daley questioned.

The girl moved closer to him, whispered close by his ear. "They didn't look around in this room when—when they put us in here, Deo," she explained. "It was almost dark, I guess, and they didn't see back in the corners. But after the moon came out, about an hour ago—look what it revealed."

Rolling over, the scout of Terror Trail saw that the moonlight streaming through the tiny square of window illuminated a pile of rusty mail armor—another skeleton of a Spaniard who had starved to death in this turret, probably shooting out of the slotlike window at besieging Indians.

"What—what good will that skeleton do us, Irene?" Daley asked.

"But can't you see? He has a sword!" pointed out the girl eagerly. "A sword in a wicker scabbard, but the scabbard has rotted away and the blade is exposed. I've been trying to saw my bonds against it, but I can't hold the sword still. But with you to hold the blade with the weight of your body, I can get my ropes off, and then I can untie you."

Daley was already rolling his tightly trussed body toward the armored skeleton under the loophole.

"I get you, Irene!" he panted. "Once we're free, we can test those bars in the window. I don't imagine they're any too strong, after all these centuries. Come on; let's hurry!"

Working feverishly, the pair started to put Irene's plan into execution. A rusty Toledo sword still hung from the skeleton's metal belt, but the flawless steel, tempered with the matchless secret which the great Toledo swordmakers have preserved throughout the ages, served as an effective, if crude, saw.

With Deo Daley resting his weight on the silver-mounted hilt, the girl was able to move her own bonds back and forth on the dull edge. While she worked, she briefly outlined her experiences. Daley's veins ran hot as he heard Irene's account of Thode's first exposure of his treachery.

Minutes dragged with agonizing slowness. Any movement, for all they knew, dawn might break over this castle of horror, to bring Don Chirlo's gang up to this turret where they were trapped. And Deo Daley knew he could not hope for mercy from Don Chirlo.

Strand by strand of the tough bonds parted, until finally Irene Garland's arms were free and she was clawing out of the coils about her feet.

Standing up, the girl flexed her stiffened fingers and knees, stepped out of the ropes, and in a few moments, with the aid of the ancient Spanish sword blade, she had chopped Deo Daley's bonds asunder and he was likewise on his feet, rubbing circulation back into his arms.

"If we escape, it'll be thanks to you, Irene!" whispered Deo Daley gratefully, stretching his cramped muscles. "Now for the actual work o' gettin' out o' this place—an' we got to hurry."

While Irene sawed free the bonds which held her still unconscious father, Deo Daley made an examination of the inch-thick bars which formed a grating over the single loophole. But when the scout turned, despair was imprinted on his face. He had found the bars, deeply embedded in solid granite, without a flaw.

"An' even if we had a saw an' could saw 'em in two, we couldn't jump out o' that window!" groaned Daley, after chinning himself over the window sill and looking out through the mellow moonlight which filled the crater in the mountains. "We are in a turret o' the outside wall. It's a hundred-foot drop, easily, to that moat."

The two stood side by side, their hearts congealing with shattered hopes. Thanks to Irene Garland's ingenuity, they were free to move about in their cell. But their freedom only added to their feeling of helplessness. And each passing second added to the peril of their situation.

"No use trying the door—it's barred, and they've left a guard outside," stated Irene, frenzy clutching her spirits. "A big Mexican—I've heard him singing to himself out there—heard him cocking his guns and whetting his knife on his boot."

Daley's fingers suddenly seized the girl's shoulders. "He's a Mexican, eh?" exclaimed the scout, in a tense whisper. "Wait, Irene! I've got an idea."

Pausing a moment, Daley made a shuffling sound with his moccasin-clad soles on the floor, followed by a loud grunt of exertion.

"These ropes tied together will get us to the ground, Irene!" exclaimed the scout, speaking in loud tones intended to reach the ears of the Mexican guard just outside the heavy door. "Out the window with you, Tex.

I guess Don Chirlo overlooked the window."

Almost instantly, there sounded from without the startled thud of high boot heels against the stone floor outside, blended with a grunt of astonishment, a Mexican oath, and a jangle of spurs:

"Hurry, the guard's comin'!" yelled Daley once more, at the same time clapping a hand to Irene's mouth to stifle her gasp of astonishment and wonder. "There! We'll make it!"

Wood scraped against wood, as the Mexican guard jerked aside the heavy bar of the turret door. And an instant later, he was pushing through the doorway, gun barrel jutting before him, the wide whites of his eyes glowing in the moonbeams.

Smack! The full weight of Deo Daley's muscular body was behind the solid punch which caught the Mexican squarely on the chin-point.

The outlaw groaned and collapsed, but his falling body was caught by Deo Daley's waiting arms. Before the six-gun could fall from the guard's nerveless fingers, Irene Garland had darted down to snatch it into her own grasp.

"Clever, Deo!" gasped the girl, as the scout laid the guard's unconscious body out on the turret floor, and deftly frisked his clothes to find another .45 and a bowie knife in a sheath in the Mexican's boot.

"Quick! We've no time to waste!" breathed the young frontiersman, jamming the six-gun into his own empty holster. "I'll carry your father. We've got to get out o' this turret!"

Down the steps of the tower they went, through gloom thick enough to press against their eyeballs. Draped over Daley's shoulder was the unconscious form of old Tex Garland. Side by side, the two escaping prisoners descended the stairway, palms sliding on the stone banister rail, until they came to the heavy oaken door opening on the castle's courtyard.

The girl pressed against the door, but it did not yield. With a gasp, Daley put down Garland's body and crashed his shoulder against the wooden panels. But it was as solid as the wall.

"It's barred on the outside!" groaned Deo Daley, despair tightening his throat. "Chirlo was takin' no chances o' that Mex guard leavin' to get a drink."

Panic clawed at their souls, as they found themselves doomed to heartbreaking defeat on the very threshold of escape. Through cracks in the huge door, they could hear sounds of revelry coming from the castle, where Don Chirlo and Curt Thode were celebrating with their evil gang.

Once the girl and the scout, pushed against the barred door with trembling bodies, caught the highpitched guffaws of Curt Thode, and both went pale with anger.

"Something drastic has got to be done, an' pronto!" rasped Deo Daley, carrying Garland's body back in the shadows. "Come here, Irene! You an' your father hide under this stairway where it's good an' dark. I'll be back soon."

"What—where are you going, Deo?" the girl cried anxiously, clinging to his hands as he forced her back under the first flight of steps, where he had lain her father. "Don't leave us!"

"They'll be coming for us any minute, Irene," insisted the young scout, pressing the loaded six-gun into the girl's hands. "I've got to look for a window out of this tower."

With the words, Deo Daley was gone, running desperately up the curving steps. At the first landing, a narrow loophole window presented itself—a window which did not open on the outer side of the turret tower.

Through the opening Daley pulled his body, to find that this window overlooked the gray, slate-plate roof of the castle wall. Like a phantom in the moonlight, the scout of Terror Trail wriggled out of the window, clung by his hands to the sill, and dropped ten feet to land light as a cat on the roof of the wall.

It was weird, alone on the streetlike roof of the square wall which fenced in the castle of gold. Across the shadow-loaded court plaza, the castle was a witch's painting in the light of a butter-colored moon which beamed through the pines.

Black smoke was tumbling from a castle chimney, ruddy sparks boiling toward the heavens. Daley could hear the wind moaning in the notched battlements of the walls about him. Off to the east, the sky above the opening of this craterlike pit in the wild mountain range was beginning to pale, promising a quick dawn.

With desperation lending speed to his cramped limbs, Deo Daley ran to the nearby parapet and leaned over. His heart turned into a granny knot as he peered down through sickening space at the stagnant moat which girdled the castle. From this level, it was more than a sixty-foot drop to the ground. And the granite-blocked wall was steeper than a fly could climb.

With despair deepening within his veins, the scout made a circuit of the four sides of the fencelike wall. But each step brought fresh defeat; there was not a single door entering any stairway through the roof; no skylights, and no entrances into any of the four turrets which cornered the wall inclosure.

Greasy with cold sweat, Deo Daley glanced about. Towering between him and the setting moon, the round tombstone of the great central pinnacle of the *Alcazar de los Ladrones* seemed to meet the star-scattered sky. Round and smooth-walled it rose, like a huge pipe surmounted by a battlement and a flagstaff.

Upon the top of that spire where the pirate flag fluttered in the breeze, the bones of Don Picadero himself molded on the stones.

Suddenly Deo Daley clasped his fists, clamped his mouth into a firm, hard line. He glanced toward the turret in the bottom of which cowered the girl he loved. He could not even get back to her, now. The window through which he had leaped was too high to catch with even a superhuman leap.

For their sake, he must take the desperate chance, put into execution the risky plan which had taken seed in his brain.

Day was only a half hour away. Dawn would bring doom. The span of night was at an end. Don Chirlo's men would come for their prisoners as soon as the light of day illuminated the tortures they had prepared for them.

"I—I *must* do it!"

Taking a deep breath, Deo Daley ran to the battlements of the south wall of the castle, climbed to the edge, and stood for a moment like a poised statue on the very brink of the parapet.

Far below, under the overhang of the outbuilt masonry rimming the castle walls, the stale, scum-padded moat made a ditch of green ink in the spectral moonlight which flooded this unreal scene out of some ancient storybook.

Palms together, knees springing, Deo Daley dived out into space, his body dropping like a plummet while the mossy stone walls of the Alcazar whistled by him and the stagnant moat whizzed up to meet him with incredible speed. Would it be deep—or shallow?

Only the startled chacalaca bird who peered from its nest in a crumbling niche of the walls witnessed the end of that amazing dive of death.

Splash! Sheets of spray shot out as the scout's body bulleted through the scum-filmed water.

Lather rode the widening ripples, gradually closing over the spot where Deo Daley had vanished into the inky depths. Rich mud roiled off the ditch bottom. The wrinkled surface of the water was ironed smooth again.

Minutes passed, but the watching bird in its nest far up the tower wall saw no fresh ripples disturbing the moat's surface. Far away, outside this hole of horror in the mountain wilderness, a questing timber wolf bayed a death song at the setting moon.

PICADERO'S GHOST

A DRUNKEN ORGY was reaching its lurid climax in the banquet hall lobby inside the *Alcazar de los Ladrones.* All night it had lasted, as the outlaws celebrated their victory.

It was enough to make the grisly skeletons who had inhabited the grim death castle for nearly half a thousand forgotten years, collect their time-corroded bones together and scale a moonbeam to escape the place.

Thode slopped down another long drink of Mexican *tequila,* and swayed beside Don Chirlo as the scar-scribbled bandit leader stood with arms behind his back, peering up the flame-flickered stairs to where the oil painting of Don Picadero was dimly outlined in the glare of the roaring fireplace.

"Don Picadero is enjoying this," chuckled the outlaw king, jerking his head in the direction of the painting. "The artist who made that picture was good, no? Ah, Thode—look! It looks so natural, Don Picadero almost wants to join us in our fiesta!"

Thode passed a hand over his eyes, tottered on his feet, and gazed up at the picture a moment. Then he began struggling with the cork of his *tequila* bottle.

"A natural painting, yes," went on Chirlo, grinning. "Don Picadero looks natural enough to—" Suddenly an amazing change swept over Don Chirlo's face. His mahogany skin drained to the hue of stale cheese. His trembling hands unlaced from behind his back, and seized Curt Thode by the arm.

"Look, Thode! Do you see eet? Don Picadero—he ees *alive*!"

Curt Thode looked once, and what he saw turned him ice-sober and buttered his face with sweat. For the moldy, peeling canvas painting was stirring with life!

It was no alcohol dream, what he saw. For the other outlaws saw it, too. Silence suddenly crammed the shouts and echoes back down the throats of the assembled crooks, as they stared up at the picture at the head of the stairway.

And then confusion broke loose like an exploding bomb. For Don Picadero was stepping down out of his picture frame, the faded plumage on his hat bobbing, one hand stealing to the gold-hilted sword at his belt!

It was impossible, yet it was true. Down the steps of that banquet-hall stairway came Don Picadero, on feet that made no sound. just as he had lived and breathed in this ill-fated Alcazar, more than three hundred years before this wild night.

Apaches leaped to their feet out of drunken stupors. They stared wildly at the approaching ghost of the long-dead Spaniard who was now halfway down the steps. Then they yelped like coyotes and sprinted for the doors.

"Chirlo. It can't be Picadero!"

Curt Thode brushed a hand across a face that was the color of rotted cowhide. Then he broke his spell, batted his eyes, and turned to flee.

At the same instant, the ghost of Terror Trail Castle vented a soul-chilling madman's laugh, and tested the springy Toledo sword blade in his two hands.

For the first time in his long career of crime, Don Chirlo felt terror clutch at his stern and brutal heart. With a bawl of panic, the big black-clad outlaw turned on his heels to race like a doomed soul for the outer door of the castle.

"Ha-a-a-a!" The laugh that wrenched from the ghost's lips as he reached the foot of the stairs was something from a witch's throat. The sword blade flashed as Don Picadero headed at a dead run in pursuit of the fleeing outlaws who jammed the exit.

A burly outlaw shook himself out of a drunken sleep and bounded to his feet, in Picadero's path. Then his hands clawed a pair of six-guns from his holsters.

Brrang! Brram! Bullets glanced off the stone-flagged floor at Don Picadero's feet, tore stone chips off the stairs, clanged musically as they punctured a crested shield on a wall.

Before the terrorized outlaw could trigger the smoking Colts at closer range, the phantom swordsman was upon him like a thunderbolt. The wire-thin sword blade sank through the ruffian's stomach and out his back, impaling him like a darning needle punched through a potato.

The outlaw wilted as Don Picadero drew the sword out, dripping blood. The blade flashed a red arc in the firelight as the amazing specter charged on through the curtained door, down the steps, and out of the castle.

Across the skeleton-strewn grass floor of the courtyard Picadero chased the outlaws. Yelling, stumbling, picking themselves up, they streamed through the outer gate of the *Alcazar de los Ladrones* like a milling herd of crazed steers.

Seconds after the last outlaw had bounded like a cannon ball out of the black castle gate, Don Picadero appeared in the moonlight at the portal's edge. His teeth were exposed in a flashing smile under the reddish-brown, spike-tipped mustaches as he paused, sword flashing, legs outspread.

Crash! The rotten drawbridge collapsed under the weight of the fleeing outlaws.

A dozen of them piled into the water with a drenching splash, and scrambled like bugs out on the muggy bank. The few who were trapped on the inner bank sloshed and clawed their way to the other side like a flock of alley cats dumped into a sewer main.

With a laugh, Don Picadero turned and vanished back into the courtyard of the Castle of Thieves.

Far out in the middle of the dawn-lit pasture which spread like a devil's lawn about the castle, Don Chirlo brought his headlong flight to a stop, as reason conquered his frenzy.

Sense was flowing back into his crafty brain. He was no coward, and he was cunning. How, he reasoned, could a ghost of Don Picadero return to this castle after three hundred years? It was absurd. And

Don Chirlo was not drunk.

"Back, hombres! Someone has been tricking us!" yelled the outlaw king, drawing his silver-mounted six-guns and waving them frantically in the faces of the drenched men who were galloping past him, eyes bulging, lungs wheezing as they sprinted like antelope for the underground river which would get them safely out of this crater filled with walking demons of the past.

But Don Chirlo's shouts were in vain. His band of crooks was a superstitious, ignorant mob. They had seen enough. They had witnessed an oil painting come to life, watched one of their number driven through and through by a ghostly sword blade.

They would face certain death against blazing sixguns with a taunting laugh, but when it came to fighting a phantom swordsman in a moonlight-flooded battleground—no!

"All right, you cowards, I'll go back myself!" bawled Don Chirlo, gathering his courage about him like a cloak. "I'll show this masquerading fool—"

Ten steps toward the castle Don Chirlo took, and then he stood stock-still. For now came the climax of the maddest drama ever enacted here below on earth! Out of the gate of the castle wall there suddenly appeared the ghost of Dan Picadero, astride a snow-white horse, and carrying a glittering shield! A prancing, white-maned animal, snorting and pawing, while chain mail clinked and a lance was a glittering white needle in the morning glow!

"The white hoss! My bullets won't hurt Don Picadero now!" the words came through Don Chirlo's chattering teeth. "It's real! *Caramba*!"

Don Chirlo's backbone suddenly turned to melted

wax. The six-guns dropped out of his palms. His eyes protruded like a pair of white marbles. His tongue went dry, and his veins turned to water.

With a husky scream of terror, Don Chirlo turned and sped across the green grassland after his departed gang.

Back at the edge of the smashed drawbridge, the ghost of Don Picadero sat astride his white horse, threw back his head, and laughed loud and long as the morning sun climbed up behind the pine-hung rim rocks, to herald a new day.

The ghost whipped off his ancient plumed hat, to expose the good-natured face of Deo Daley, the scout of Terror Trail. Tossing his shield and lance aside, the "ghost" of Don Picadero reined his horse about and rode back through the iron-bolted, pine-log gate of the castle of gold.

"It worked, eh, Gunpowder?" choked the scout of Terror Trail, as he dismounted and unsaddled the horse. "We have the castle to ourselves now!"

Running to the wall door of Irene Garland's prison, Deo Daley unbarred it, and moments later he was leading the two prisoners out into the dawn-lighted courtyard. They were in time to see Gunpowder, free of saddle and blanket, shake his body like a dog. Instantly a burst of white powder blossomed in the morning air, and the horse's body was revealed as ebony in the first gray beams of dawn.

Then Gunpowder lay down in the grass and rolled. When he got to his feet with a snort, the ghost horse of Don Picadero was no longer white. Once again, Gunpowder was Deo Daley's coal-black cayuse.

"I'll never forget how they busted up their celebration when I stepped out from that picture frame!" chuckled Deo Daley, as he led Tex and Irene Garland into the wreckage-littered lobby of the banquet room. "I'd taken the clothes off o' Picadero's corpse."

They stood a moment, looking at the liquor spilled on the floor, at the shattered dishes and overturned furniture, the motionless corpse and the flickering fire. The scout of Terror Trail dropped an arm about the shoulders of the smiling girl and her grizzled father.

"Now we're safe, an' Chirlo an' Thode are out there without food or horses," he chuckled. "As soon as we get caught up on food an' sleep, folks, we'll start in spectin' this castle o' Don Picadero's. Somewhere inside it is a heap o' Spanish treasure, an' it'll be ours."

PLOTTING REVENGE

DON CHIRLO unscrewed the bolt which held together the barrel and stock of his .30-.3o rifle and carefully packed the dismantled gun inside the oilskin slicker which contained his clothing and six-gun belts.

Beside him on the bank of the Rio Torcido, his spy, Curt Thode, was tying a lariat rope around a similar waterproof bundle.

"This looks like a harebrained idea to me, Chirlo—swimmin' under water past an armed guard!" protested Thode, stripping off his undershirt so that he was now prepared for his dive into the chilly mountain waters. "An' from the looks the rest o' the gang is givin' us, they ain't expectin' to see us alive ag'in after we goes inside o' the mouth o' the Blue Skull!"

Don Chirlo, stripped to reveal a brown-skinned

100

chest slabbed with muscles, powerful thighs as big as spruce logs, and long, hair-weeded arms, got to his feet and tucked the oilskin bundle under one elbow.

"Bah—that ees why I am the boss of thees gang, an' they are but keelers, gun hawks!" scorned the half-breed crook, turning to scan the silent crowd of cold-eyed men who were assembled there at the base of La Crescenta Canyon.

"Right this minute, Daley's in there gloatin' because he's found the Castle o' Thieves, I bet!" grunted Curt Thode, picking up his knot-bound slicker package. "But he's got a guard at the other end o' this cavern, Chirlo, who'll see us swimmin' by an' gun us out like otter."

The scar-scribbled face of the outlaw twisted in a fiendish grin. Ever since Curt Thode had tipped him off that Deo Daley was on the trail of Spanish gold, Chirlo and his gang had pursued Daley's expedition. Now, on the very threshold of the lost *Alcazar de los Ladrones,* he was not going to admit defeat. Chirlo was of sterner stripe.

"An' after we git in, how are we goin' to git in the castle?" demanded Thode, struggling to change Chirlo's mind. "We can't—"

"Bah! My scheme ees *bueno, I* tell you!" repeated the outlaw, turning to wave a farewell to his sober-faced, worried band of crooks. "*Adios, amigos!* I weel be back pronto—as soon as I keel Deo Daley."

Mumbling their doubts, the crooks trooped forward as Don Chirlo, clutching the waterproof parcel containing his guns and clothing, dived expertly into the foaming pool at the mouth of the Blue Skull.

Thode, trembling with ill-concealed fear, followed him into the icy depths, and the two swimmers,

101

battling the slow current which sluiced out of the hole in the cliff, were soon lost to sight inside the inky jaws of the Blue Skull.

In the gloom, the two men swam for and found a ledge on one side of the grotto wall—a ledge which took them, on foot, deep into the maw of the earth. The raging of the water through the gloom beat against their eardrums, making speech impossible.

The sootlike gloom thinned a trifle as they fought through the flying spume and scrambled to the top of the stairway of water. A few yards of swimming through eddying currents brought them to an abrupt bend in the tunnel of water, and their eyes narrowed as a huge half-moon of blinding daylight smote their pupils.

Don Chirlo rasped hoarse instructions to his blanch-faced spy: "See those reeds, those tules, outside? We weel sweem under water. Eef they have a guard, he weel not see us as we come up een those tules! Let's go.

Filling his lungs with air to the bursting point, Curt Thode clutched his bundle of slicker-wrapped clothing and guns close to his chest, and dived fishlike beneath the surface of the gliding river until his knees touched bottom.

The water turned greenish as they got under the current and crept along the floor of a rocky pool. Their eyes started from their sockets.

Upon the bank, a grizzled old pioneer in buckskins sat with a rifle across his knees, his blue eyes glued to the dark throat of the cavern. He little dreamed that deep below the surface of the foam-sudsy river which glided past him, two phantomlike bodies were creeping close to the river's bottom.

Tiny splashes went unheard by the vigilant watchman at the cave's mouth, as two heads parted the water deep among the reeds which grew around a bend of the Rio Torcido's bank.

Don Chirlo and Curt Thode, releasing their pent-up breaths carefully, looked at each other in triumph as they realized they had successfully passed their first obstacle, the sentinel.

From where they hid, deep in the thicket of rushes where they were safe from detection, Chirlo and Thode could look out across the saucer of green meadowland which formed the bottom of this circular, cliff-walled pit in the mountains.

Occupying the center of the grassy basin through which the river wound its way, lifted the gray walls of the Castle of Thieves.

"We better keep swimmin' in the river all the way, Chirlo," advised Curt Thode, after the pair had rested for a few moments. "Hard tellin' but what Deo Daley an' the girl are up there on the walls, keepin' a watch out. Once we're seen, we're done for."

Nodding agreement, Chirlo followed his spy as Thode ducked beneath the surface of the river, knifed through the reeds, and swam rapidly under the surface until two more bends of the river brought them safely out of view of the guard by the cave mouth.

Coming up to breathe again, the pair floated in an eddy until they were rested. The slicker-wrapped bundles, despite the weight of their guns, assisted them in keeping afloat, until they were ready once more to continue their under-water progress.

The Rio Torcida glided between grass-hung banks, near one corner of the ancient castle, and the swimming outlaws repeated their under-water swimming laps until the darkening water told them they were under the very shadow of the walls.

The pair waited a few minutes, submerged to their armpits in the water weeds close to the bank, before venturing out on the grassy flat which lay between the river banks and the deep ditch which formed the moat about the castle.

Then, convinced that neither the scout of Terror Trail nor any of his party was watching the river, they slipped up the muddy banks, hurried noiselessly across the grass to the moat, and in a few seconds were swimming across the scummy, lily-padded moat.

Scrambling out on the shelf of dirt between moat and castle wall, the two men hurriedly untied their bundles and donned clothing, which they found had been kept almost dry during their swim.

"Now what we goin' to do, Chirlo?" demanded Curt Thode, as he strapped a cartridge belt about his waist. "We can't climb these sixty-foot walls, an' it'd be suicide to try the gate."

Don Chirlo was unconcerned as he looked up at the beetling expanse of the mossy granite walls. As he did so, he was deftly tying a couple of wraps of lariat rope about his rifle, where stock and breech met. That done, he knotted Thode's lariat to his own, making a sizable coil of pliable rope connected to the gun.

"I said my idea was *bueno!*" reminded Don Chirlo. "Watch!"

Coiling the reatas about one arm, the big outlaw took the Winchester by the stock, balanced it as he might test a javelin, and then looked upward, his smut-black eyes searching for the nearest loophole window in the castle wall.

Following Chirlo, a mystified look on his swarthy

face, Curt Thode clawed at his black sideburns and was frankly puzzled by his leader's actions. Chirlo paused when he stood directly under a window, which was about fifteen feet above them.

"Now you shall see she ees not eempossible to geet eento the *Alcazar de los Ladrones,* eef you have brains!" chuckled the outlaw, getting a good footing on the grass and taking a fresh grip on the gun. "Mebbe we try once, twice—but she work. Look!"

So saying, the outlaw drew back his arm as if he was about to hurl a spear. With terrific strength, Chirlo cast the long-barrelled rifle upward.

Like a lance, the muzzle of the Winchester rifle soared through the slotlike window, and a second later Curt Thode heard a muffled clang as the rifle fell to the floor of a room inside the walls. As he looked, Don Chirlo pulled on the rope until it became taut.

The rifle was now lodged crosswise in the window above, with steel barrel and walnut stock supporting Chirlo's weight as he tested the rope. Then, gripping the lariats firmly, he put his toes on the rough stones and started scaling the wall.

Less than a minute later, the outlaw's huge hands were hooked on the lower sill of the thick-walled opening. Panting with exertion, he got his knees to the sill and grabbed the inside wall with one hand, while the other lowered the rifle quietly to the floor. He rested a moment, then straddled the moss-grown sill.

DALEY GETS A SURPRISE

MANY TIMES IN the scout of Terror Trail's twenty-three years of adventurous living along the outer edges of America's wild Western frontier, he had been faced with crushing and utter defeat.

Each time he had accepted his lot with chin up and heart undaunted, taking it as part of his he-man game. But now, as Deo Daley made his way through the gloomy halls of the ancient castle, the thought of telling Irene Garland that the treasure expedition was a failure, after all the hair-raising risks and hardships they had suffered, was gallingly hard.

His striding moccasins made a jangling sound as they crashed into a pile of junk, and he paused, sweat bedewing his face. He knew, even without looking down, that he had tripped over the armor-dressed bones of a Spanish warrior who had been among the horde to die there in the Castle of Thieves.

All day he had been searching the castle, from the lowest compartment of the deepest dungeon keep to the highest floor of the turrets on the outer walls. No corner had gone unscanned. He had found no trace of the treasure that was supposed to rest in this castle, but he had seen plenty of gruesome skeletons.

Daley made his way along a dark corridor, shouldered through a ragged hole in the moldy, sodden draperies which curtained a doorway, and stood on the edge of the banquet hall, or lobby, of Don Picadero's amazing lost castle.

"Any luck this time, Deo? Or is the gold a myth, after all?" A girl's voice started ghosty, musical

106

echoes in the big banquet hall, and a slow flood of color mounted in Deo Daley's bronzed skin. The time had come to make his difficult announcement.

The scout shook his head as he strode out across the checkerboard floor of stone and headed for the soot-blackened fireplace of the lobby. Over by a hand-hewn table stood Irene Garland.

"I—I guess somebody either beat us to this treasure castle, or else it was a fake legend about Don Picadero hidin' any gold here, Irene," blurted out the trail scout, coming to a halt across the table from the girl. "I— I've fine-combed every crevice in this castle, from cellar to attic. An' I've found nothin' that even suggests a treasure chamber. I—I'm afraid we're licked—risked our hides for nothin'."

"I—I suppose it was one of the chances we had to take, coming to this castle," said the girl slowly, coming around the table and putting a sympathetic hand on Daley's fringed buckskin sleeve. "I—I don't care so much for—for myself. But Daddy—he's old, and when Don Chirlo destroyed our wagon train that time, it was all he had in the world, you know."

Daley fingered the cleft in his sombrero crown. His eyes avoided the girl's face, to rove about the balcony rail which rimmed all four sides of the room.

"I'll take another look through the rooms in the outer walls, Irene," sighed the scout, pressing the hand which rested against his arm. "Now that the sun's swung around to the west side o' the castle, I might be able to find somethin' I missed."

The girl returned the scout's smile, and went back to the dough she had been mixing in a tin bowl on the table.

"I'm fixing up some food to take out to Dad," she

said, dusting her fingers with snowy flour. "He's been guarding the mouth of that river all morning, you know."

Daley's white teeth flashed in a smile. "I'll make a torch out o' this fireplace wood an' have one more look—see; then I'll go out an' let your dad have a rest, Irene," he promised.

Holding the torch away from him, he headed out of the lobby, down a flight of steps, and out on a long corridor where the echoes picked up his padding steps and repeated them in uncanny whispers. Going out the outer door of the lost castle, he was grateful for the warm sunshine which poured down into the grassy courtyard of the castle.

The plaza was little more than a canyon between the square fence of stone walls which surrounded the box-like structure of the Alcazar itself. Grass had grown to hay, seeded and grown again, covering the hulks of buzzard-devoured Spanish horses and the corpses of human beings scattered here and there.

Daley made his way to a door in the base of the wall and went inside, the torch showing him a dank terrace of steps, which he climbed until he came to the corridor which girdled the entire sweep of the four walls.

A curtained doorway loomed to Daley's left, and he shuddered as he pressed aside the damp, musty folds of cloth, holding the flaming stick of wood away from the fibers.

Then an exclamation of surprise wrenched through the scout's teeth, as he stood on the threshold of the dark, sinister room.

He was standing face to face with the equally surprised figure of Don Chirlo!

Swift as the dive of a hawk after a rabbit, the arm of Deo Daley hurled the flaming torch at Chirlo's face and then plummeted toward the red stock of his holstered .45

The outlaw, surprised in the act of going out the door which the young scout had just entered, saw bleak death shining from Daley's eyes as he ducked the hastily thrown firebrand.

Whizz! Chirlo's left hand shot forth, and fingers as hard and unyielding as the fangs of a bear trap closed on the wrist of Deo Daley's gun hand as he jerked the six-gun from leather.

Br—rang! The hammer of the gun fell, and a ribbon of searing fire spouted from the black bore.

Something like a hornet sped by the bandit's cheek, and the bullet thudded into the opposite wall as Chirlo forced the smoking gun upward and aside.

The torch fell spluttering into a far corner, casting queer shadows against the curtain as the two men crashed together in a bending, writhing grapple.

There was no time for either man to think. Daley had supposed this craterlike well in the mountain range was free of the outlaws whom he had single-handedly driven out of the castle the night before.

The six-gun dropped from Daley's hand, and he bit back a cry of pain as Chirlo's tightening grip threatened to crush the wrist bones. Then both men toppled to the floor again, twisting and rolling like a tiger and a lion clasped in mortal combat.

Bullet swift, Daley's legs twisted like a nutcracker about Chirlo's middle, as the big outlaw drove three skin-smashing blows into the scout's contorted face.

Then the outlaw released his grip on Daley's crippled wrist to claw at the legs which seemed to be squeezing him into a pulp. Daley took advantage of the instant to hook his right arm in a grim headlock about the crook's post-thick neck.

Roaring like an injured bull, Don Chirlo resorted to a somersault which twisted the fight back into the corner with a blur of thrashing legs and arms.

Fists thudded against flesh, like cannon balls plunking into a wooden wall. Grunts of agony whistled through grated jaws. Sweat boiled from the pores of the fighters as Don Chirlo, by a superhuman effort, broke Daley's crushing scissor hold and writhed to his feet, snarling Spanish oaths.

The wind went from Chirlo's lungs with a grunt as Daley's uplashing feet caught him in the pit of the stomach in a common wrestler's trick. Even as the outlaw reeled aside, Deo Daley bounced to his feet, and they met toe to toe, exchanging slugging blows.

Chirlo outweighed his opponent by forty pounds of brawn, but Daley made up for his handicap by twinkling footwork and a weaving, spiderlike motion which eluded blows that would have cracked his head like a biscuit crust.

Squalling hoarsely, Don Chirlo lowered his head and smashed through a barrage of blinding punches to force Daley out of a corner and into the center of the room.

The lighter scout was forced to clinch, and they were on the floor again in a rolling tangle as they wrestled for an advantage.

Sock! Daley drove a bone-splintering blow to Chirlo's temple, and the big outlaw wilted, dazed.

Like lightning, Deo Daley was out of the bandit's clutches, swayed to his feet, and groped for his sheathed bowie knife with a trembling hand.

Don Chirlo saw death in that flashing steel blade as

he reared to his feet and clawed at his second six-gun. But Daley had anticipated the draw, and he was on Chirlo like a wolf charging a longhorn bull.

Chirlo was carried flat on his back by the scout's onslaught, and then the outlaw shot both hands up to seize Daley's arm in time to prevent the long knife from hewing through his ribs.

Daley's knees were pinning the big man to the floor. Sweat burst from the scout's pulsing temples as he forced his knife arm lower, inch by inch, every ounce of his tiger-like strength pitted against the springlike resistance of Chirlo's straining muscles.

No cry for mercy escaped Chirlo's lips. He went purple with exertion, his scars showing lividly, but he was no coward. The knife blade trembled with the tension as Daley, a chance to snatch victory from long odds now in sight, put his weight on his effort and brought the steel point closer and closer to the outlaw's heaving chest. Whenever the break came, the stroke would fall.

Thus it was that Deo Daley's jutting eyes did not detect the shadow that suddenly filled the open window behind them. Nor did Don Chirlo, fighting for his life to hold that sinking blade in air, see the leering features of Curt Thode as his spy hauled his body over the window sill by means of the rifle=held rope.

Daley's head cranked about as he heard Curt Thode picking up the Winchester .30-.3o by the muzzle. Using the gun for a club, Thode brought down the wooden stock with a crunching thud.

The scout of Terror Trail slumped like a dead man over Don Chirlo's quivering form. The knife dropped from his fingers, and fell harmlessly on the outlaw's heaving chest.

Gasping for breath, Don Chirlo shook off the scout's limp weight and climbed to his feet. For a moment the two men regarded each other, standing over the body of their mutual enemy.

Don Chirlo spoke first. "We—we better get out of here!" said the trembling outlaw, recovering his fallen six-guns and tromping callously on the inert form of his opponent. "Somebody might o' heard the shot— Tex Garland or the *señorita.*"

"An' we'll take this skunk with us!" grated Curt Thode, picking up Daley's body as if it were a sack. "I ain't goin' to be through with him for a while yet— else I'd a shot 'im in the back just now."

Bruised and battered from his recent battle, Don Chirlo picked up Daley's torch and lurched out of the curtained doorway, with Thode following him to the corridor. Just ahead, a stairway dropped away into an ink-black opening.

"Down here—until I've collected my wind!" wheezed the outlaw leader, heading down the stair with his torch. "I got a score to settle with that young scout!"

THE CHEST OF DEATH

IRENE GARLAND finished dishing up her father's meal of beans, coffee, hearth-baked bread, bacon and honey. She arranged it carefully on a circular-shaped shield which she had taken from a wall rack to use for a tray, and headed in the direction of the outdoors.

"I can't bear to tell Daddy that there isn't any gold here," she murmured, as she carried the steaming tray of food out of the castle portal and headed across the grass-grown courtyard. "If—"

Boom! The muffled sound of a shot caused Irene to stop in her tracks.

"That—that sounded like a shot!" gasped Irene, her spine suddenly turning cold. "I wonder if they're attacking Daddy—"

Setting down the tray of food, Irene Garland headed across the castle plaza, her knife palmed in one small brown hand.

And then her acute ears picked up the sound of swearing men and thudding blows, as she passed a doorway in the huge inner wall of the fortifications surrounding the *Alcazar de los Ladrones* like a great, thick fence!

"Then it must be Deo—in trouble!" exclaimed the girl, forgetting possible danger to herself as she darted into the dark opening and groped her way up the stairs, hands fluttering in front of her face like startled birds winging their way through the dark. The instant she gained the corridor above, she realized that the sounds of a melee were issuing from one of the many doors facing both sides of the hallway.

Her heart raced, making every nerve in her body tingle. Gripping her knife harder, Irene flattened out against the wall, and with one sweat-moist hand sliding along the cold, dank stones, commenced groping her way down the murky corridor.

She had soon traveled the entire width of the castle and was turning the corner. From time to time she caught the faint jingling of spurs, the crashing of straining boots on stone, the grunt of hard-breathing, fast-punching men.

It seemed incredible that Deo Daley could possibly have encountered any foe inside the castle. The outlaws of Don Chirlo were all driven outside the crater, and could get into the castle only by coming through the narrow cave entrance, which her father was guarding. And Irene had too much confidence in her rugged old father's ability to handle a Winchester rifle to think that any crook could have sneaked into the castle basin unseen.

Suddenly the girl fell back, stifling a gasp of surprise. Not forty yards down the hallway ahead of her, a light was glimmering, throwing weaving shadows out of a curtained door entrance!

Cringing back in shadow, hand tense on knife haft, Irene saw the towering, *gaucho*-costumed Don Chirlo back out of that doorway, holding the torch which she had seen Deo Daley take out of the fireplace not fifteen minutes before.

Sick despair froze Irene's heart into a lump as she next saw the tall, lean figure she recognized as the treacherous Curt Thode emerge from the door, carrying the limp form of Daley!

In a trice, Irene read the scout's fate. He had gone to search the wall's rooms, in one last desperate effort to locate the fabled gold coffers of Don Picadero. Somehow, Don Chirlo and Curt Thode had been hiding, and had pounced out upon him. It was too bewildering to attempt to figure out.

For a moment, the impulse to flee seized the girl as she watched the two outlaws, painted red by the flickering blaze of the torch, standing in the middle of the corridor, mumbling to each other. Then they vanished through the opposite wall, down into some unseen opening in the pitchy gloom.

As she saw the flicker of the light fading, she knew that they were taking Deo Daley down a flight of stairs.

Terror and her love for the young scout battled for a place in her soul; and her faithful loyalty won.

Gripping the bowie hilt with fresh courage reviving her heart, Irene Garland stooped and unbuckled her noisy spurs, and then ran like a deer down the black corridor.

Her groping hands located the head of the stairs down which the outlaws had carried the scout. Her heart was a swelling knot in her throat as she headed down the stairway, forcing her way through foul-smelling blackness as thick as paint.

The stair reached a landing, and she bumped against a moss-padded wall. Then she turned, and saw faint shimmerings of ruddy light far below, reflected around another bend in the stair steps.

Down the second flight she ran, gaining another landing which she knew must be far below the level of the ground outside. The third pitch of steps was at a sharp angle, and seemed to penetrate the very core of the earth. It was damp and cool as a cistern.

Fifty feet below her she could see the shadows of the two outlaws silhouetted against a solid wall of granite rock. She realized by that sign that these mysterious stairs left the castle wall, tunneled deep under the plaza courtyard, and tapped an underground cellar which had been hewn out of solid bedrock.

Breathing fast, but with one tiny fist clutching her knife, Irene Garland slipped down the last stretch of stair steps and found herself cringing in a shadowfilled corner of a dungeon far below the Castle of Thieves.

The outlaws, with their torch, were around the next corner, but the girl decided to collect her wits before venturing forth.

As her eyes became accustomed to the eerie

darkness, she saw that the tomblike, rock-sealed room was filled with strange machinery which she could not understand. Racks and platforms, draped with cobwob meshes; wheels and ladders, chests and debris. It was like the devil's workshop, full of strange instruments.

Then, like a flash, she knew where she was. It was the torture room of Don Picadero—the bottom of a minelike shaft under the central dungeon keep of the Alcazar, in which all the dread engines of ancient Spanish cruelty were stored.

Deo had found them, told her about them. Only this morning he had gone down these same steps in his futile search for the gold of Don Picadero. He had found no gold, but he had come back upstairs to horrify Irene's ears with the description of the mysterious torture devices he had found down here in this room.

The low voices of the outlaws snapped her back to her senses. Scarcely daring to breathe, the girl crept to the corner of the little hallway at the foot of the stairs and peered cautiously around the corner.

Chirlo and Thode had placed Deo Daley in a great device resembling a gallows, except that his outspread arms were inside rusty iron clamps, and an iron collar had been bolted about his head. It was a Castillian whipping post, in which the victim is powerless to move. An ancient and brittle cat-o'-nine-tails hung from its corroded brass hook on the whipping-post frame.

"We'll leave him here to come to his senses!" came the fiendish voice of Curt Thode. "No use larrupin' him with the whip until he kin feel it, eh, Chirlo?"

Kneeling before the fiendish apparatus, in the act of clamping Daley's ankles to the base of the machine,

116

were Thode and Chirlo, backs to the girl. Taking advantage of the moment, she slipped on out into the open and hid herself behind a great structure of wood which she recognized as a rack of the Middle Ages.

"There, he's fixed!" boomed Chirlo as the two got to their feet. "Come on; let's get out o' here an' find the girl!"

The two outlaws were turning away from the limp body of the scout, and Irene Garland, cringed back in the shadows, felt her face suddenly go white. She had trapped herself in that den of torture! She could not possibly get to the stairway without being seen!

The outlaws were coming closer, Don Chirlo holding the flaming torch aloft. It would be suicide, she knew, to face both men with only a knife for defense. There was nothing to do but hide.

"Yeah, we'll find the *señorita*!" agreed Thode. "An' we'll kill her down here on these things they used for torture, too!"

Gasping with terror as she realized she would be discovered as soon as the two had carried the torch past the torture rack where she was hiding, the girl looked frantically about.

Her gaze landed on an ancient chest the size of a trunk, made of Chinese camphor wood and richly engraved. The lid was thrown back perhaps by Deo Daley that morning, on the chance it might contain treasure—and from where she crouched, pressed back in the shadows, Irene could see that the chest was empty.

Taking a desperate chance of being seen by the approaching crooks, Irene slipped noiselessly as a phantom to the chest, stepped inside, and lowered the brown carved top to shut the box, only an instant before the revealing light of Chirlo's torch bathed the corner where she had hidden with dancing light.

Holding her breath, the girl trembled inside the chest, panic seizing her as she heard the steps of the two crooks suddenly stop, not two feet from the box. Had they discovered her?

Irene's fingers crept up to pull the top of the trunk-like box tighter, and as she did so, a faint click sounded inside the wall of the trunk beside her ear.

With a moan of horror, Irene knew the alarming truth. The ancient lock of the chest had snapped shut. She was sealed in an air-tight coffin, to smother!

Don Chirlo's scar-seamed face frowned under the dancing flicker of his smoky torch as he reached forth a booted toe to kick the side of a coffee-brown camphor-wood chest.

"A box, Thode," grunted the half-breed, shifting the torch to his other hand. "Who knows but what eet ees feel' weeth the gold o' Don Picadero, no?"

The two outlaws looked at each other, their serpent-like eyes brightening with greed as they glanced again at the carved wooden case at their feet. Stooping, Curt Thode gripped the heavy handles of the trunk, tugged. One corner of the chest came off the floor.

"*Muy* heavy, Chirlo!" announced the spy, his teeth flashing in a brutal smile. "Let's carry it upstairs an' look inside it—after we've finished findin' an' killin' Irene Garland!"

Lending ready assent to the Army man's suggestion, Dan Chirlo took one of the handles, and together the two powerful men carried the casket-like chest into the hallway and up the winding flights of stairs toward the courtyard above.

Back in the torture den, Deo Daley was blinking

himself back to consciousness, only to find himself helplessly locked in the collars and anklets and wrist bands of the ancient whipping post.

"*Caramba*, thees box must contain much gold!" wheezed the bandit king as he lowered his end of the box to swab sweat off his waxen features as they reached the top of the stairs. "We weel take eet out een the open an' look at eet, *no es verdad?*"

Chirlo discarded his torch, and the two outlaws lifted the heavy chest once more. They made their way to the door leading off the corridor to the sunswept plaza outside. There, with grunts of relief, they proceeded to dump it roughly to the grass, and stood beside it, mopping moisture off their necks.

Thode, kneeling in front of the corroded brass lock of the trunk, tugged at it with his bare hands, then unholstered his six-gun and tried to jimmy the lid open with his gun barrel.

"Bah! Thees ees the way to open eet!" the big outlaw leader said gruffly, shoving Thode roughly aside and hefting a big .45 in his other hand. "We weel blow the lock open, *si!*"

Br-r-rang! The .45 roared out, echoes clamoring between the walls of the castle and its surrounding fortifications.

The bullet gouged a deep dent in the brass lock, but the heavy metal plate resisted puncture by the leaden slug, which went whining off into space to glance off a battlement and tear slate flakes from a turret's tepee-shaped roof.

"Ah! Now she weel open!" guffawed the outlaw, pouching his smoking Colt and getting his brittle fingernails under the edge of the trunk lid. "Now mebbe we see the—"

Curt Thode glanced fearfully around, his gun drawn. "An' you've prob'ly roused of man Garland an' the gal, so's they'll come runnin' to see what the shot's about!" grunted Thode uneasily. "Here, let me give you a hand."

Together the two tugged at the box lid. With a grating of shattered lock fixtures, the camphor-wood cover of the ancient trunk swung upward on corroded and protesting hinges.

There, cringing in the bottom of the trunk, was the doubled-up form of a big-eyed girl!

With a scream of terror, Irene Garland was out of the case like a jack-in-the-box that has lost its fastenings. Don Chirlo fell back with a grunt of surprise as the girl darted catlike under his arms and fled for the outer gate of the castle walls.

In two quick darts, Curt Thode caught up with the fleeing girl. His leg tripped her flying ankles. Then both his arms seized her elbows, forced them back behind her shoulder blades, wrenched the bowie knife from her fingers before she could get it into play.

Gasping with terror, the flaming-eyed girl writhed in the grasp of Curt Thode as he dragged her back before Don Chirlo, who stood with arms akimbo beside the opened chest.

"We no find gold, but the *señorita* leeves een thees box, eh?" boomed the big outlaw, glancing into the dusty trunk and back at the quivering prisoner in Thode's grasp. "'*Sta bueno,* Thode!"

The girl ceased her struggles as Curt Thode twisted her arm with a force that wilted her. A dirty palm stifled her cry of agony. The traitor craned his neck to glance through the open gates of the castle, to where sunlight turned the stagnant waters of the moat into a plate of silver. Then his glance soared up to the top of the buttressed walls.

"I have an idea, Chirlo!" exclaimed Curt Thode, his eyes narrowing like a demon's as they flicked from moat to wall top. "We will put her back in the box, carry her to the top of the wall, and throw her into the moat."

A quick light kindled in Chirlo's snakish eyes as the meaning of Thode's scheme penetrated his poisonous brain.

"Why not?" agreed the outlaw leader, suddenly jerking out his gun. "An' the box, she weel be fool of holes. She weel seenk queekly."

So saying, Chirlo lashed out a boot toe to tip the camphor-wood case over on its side, its lid snapping shut once more like the jaws of an alligator.

Holding the gun muzzle close to the wooden bottom of the case, Don Chirlo triggered six slugs through the tough wood. When he had finished, the bottom and sides of the chest resembled a nutmeg grater, filled with splinter-collared holes.

Irene was too weak from terror to struggle as she felt Curt Thode lift her limp form and cram it once more into the camphor-wood box. Then horror flooded her soul and she struggled frantically as the lid was crushed down on her head and pushing hands. Through a jagged bullet hole, she saw the grassy bed of the courtyard gliding by as the outlaws lifted her coffin and commenced carrying it. Then she was conscious of going through the castle door into total darkness.

The trunk tilted, jammering her body to one end of the box as it was lugged at a jouncing gait upstairs. Five minutes later, Don Chirlo and Curt Thode had carried their human freight to the battlements which edged the streetlike roof of the sixty-foot walls.

The muffled screams of the girl in the bullet-riddled chest made the men guffaw with cruel mirth as they tested the lid of the box to see that it was snapped securely shut and locked. Then, squatting, they put their arms beneath it and slid the trunk into the square slot of the battlemented parapet.

"*Adios,* Irene!" taunted Curt Thode, his lips to a bullet hole. "We're throwin' you off the wall, into the moat. If you'd a been smart an' taken me instead o' that tramp Daley, this wouldn't a happened."'

An' the scout o' Terror Trail, he die soon, too!" cut in Don Chirlo as the two shoved on the end of the trunk.

The girl's screams ceased as the trunk teetered for an awful moment on the brink of the castle wall. Then, with a final shove, Chirlo and Thode sent it toppling over into empty space.

Down, down, down, whirling end over end, the trunk dwindled through sickening space. There was a resounding splash as the box struck the surface of the moat, rainbows playing into the dancing sheets of spray as it sank.

Up it came to the surface again, then tilted crazily as water gushed through the bullet-shattered sides and bottom. Spinning like a block in a whirlpool, the crate containing the body of Irene Garland vanished in a froth of foam to the bottom of the stagnant moat.

A few bubbles fought their way to the freedom of the surface, and then the two outlaws watching from above saw the water go smooth again. There were no more bubbles . . .

WATER-FILLED BOX

GRIZZLED OLD TEX GARLAND, posted on sentry duty before the mouth of the cavern which marked the only possible means of entering the crater of the Castle of Thieves, rummaged through the pockets of his buckskins for corncob pipe and tobacco.

In a few minutes, smoke was purling through his brush of salt-gray whiskers, and he settled himself down to continue his watch over the black mouth of the cave.

"I'd like to see that army o' Dan Chirlo's try to git through here!" exploded the old man, his twinkling eyes shining inside their folded pouches of seamy lid. He rubbed an apple-hued cheek with a horny knuckle. "I reckon by now they're kitin' it back acrost Destruction Desert, bein' as we got all their grub inside o' the castle. They'd starve to death if they stayed—"

The crash of a gunshot welled out of the *Alcazar de los Ladrones,* and the old Watchman bounced to his feet in alarm, and hobbled to the top of a grassy knoll from which he could see both the cavern mouth and the castle at the same time.

"That's the second shot I've heard comin' from that place this mornin'!" grunted the old man, chewing his pipestem nervously. "But Deo Daley an' Irene couldn't be in no trouble, 'cause them crooks is all outside."

Still, the old veteran of the frontier trails was worried. He was sure that no outlaws had got past him, but who knew the dangers which lay in that unlucky castle that had been a slaughterhouse once upon a time? "There might be one o' them drunken crooks was

123

in the castle from yesterday, where we didn't see 'im!" the thought suggested itself to Tex Garland's troubled brain. "Still, I can't leave my look-out post to find out."

Brooding anxiously, the veteran paced about, blowing a smoke screen out of his beard, his eyes roving nervously from the castle to the mouth of the cave.

Suddenly, the sound of a girl's scream wafted to Tex Garland's aged ears, and he spun about. And then a sight met his gaze which paralyzed him, rooting him helpless to his tracks.

He saw two men lugging a box-like object along the roof of the castle wall facing the Rio Torcido. And he distinctly heard screams issuing in muffled tones out of that brown coffin!

Garland's tongue froze to the roof of his mouth as he recognized the two men as Chirlo and Thode. Then he saw them shove the box off into space with jeering cries.

Garland's faded eyes bugged out and rolled downward in their lids as they followed the plummeting flight of that box to the moat below. He saw the fount of water erupt over the box, saw the two outlaws turn to each other with hearty guffaws as the chest sank in the bubbling ditch.

Not until the two crooks, looking like black ants from that distance, had disappeared behind the notched battlements did Tex Garland gather his bones together and move.

Then, all thoughts of the unguarded tunnel vanished from his reeling brain. Taking a tight grip on his Winchester, he bolted like a yearling colt for the Castle of Thieves.

Like a brown ghost with a bannering scrub of beard,

the old man vaulted hummocks and tore through waist-high grass as he sprinted for the spot where he had seen that box plunge into the moat.

Poised on the very verge of the moat, Tex Garland caught himself as he remembered that he could not swim a stroke. It would be suicide for him to dive after that crate and confirm his horrifying hunch that the body of his daughter had been inside.

It was a mad, horrible nightmare, spotting those two outlaw leaders on the roof wall above. How had they got past him? Was there another entrance to that cylinder-shaped hole in the mountains? Had his eyes tricked him into thinking he had seen a box hurtling down into the moat? But it must be true, for his head was clear and his eyes powerful despite his sixty-odd years.

"I got to git Daley! My girl's drowndin' down there—"

Babbling a prayer through his fluttering beard, Tex Garland scrambled across the smashed wreckage of what had once been a log drawbridge, leaping a six-foot gap to cling with his nails to the opposite side of the shattered wooden span.

Then he was scuttling through the castle gate, heading across the courtyard at a lumbering gallop.

A faint voice came to his ears: "Irene! Look out! There's crooks in here!"

It was Deo Daley's voice, and the call issued from a nearby door, muted as if it came from a great distance. Through the door Garland sped, snatched up the glowing torch he found on the corridor floor where it had been dropped by Don Chirlo. With the speed of his passage fanning flame from the charred torch, Tex Garland followed the sounds of Deo Daley's warning yells down into the underground dungeon.

Risking his neck as he dived down twisting stairways, Tex Garland was a chattering maniac as he followed his spark-trailing torch into the torture den where the scout of Terror Trail shed sweat and writhed at his iron bonds.

"Irene! They've dumped her alive into the moat!" squalled Tex Garland as he jerked rusted pins out of the collar band which circled Deo Daley's neck. "We got to help her—quick!"

Tex Garland's grief-stricken brain went blank for a time, and he did not remember the details of freeing the scout of Terror Trail from the iron straps of the whipping post, nor the mad race against death as they sped up the stairs, out of the dungeon, and headed at a dead run across the sunny courtyard of the castle.

By the barest of seconds, the two escaped meeting Curt Thode and Don Chirlo, who were just descending the stairs out of the turret which they had climbed to dispose of Irene Garland.

"There! It was there they threw her!" jabbered Tex Garland as he and Deo Daley slid to a stop in the water grasses rimming the inside of the stagnant, smelly moat. "She's down there!"

The scout peeled off his bandoleer and six-gun belt. Then his lithe body made an arc through the air as he sprang off the bank to cleave through a thick bed of lily pads and vanish under the scummy water.

Daley kept his lips tight against his teeth to prevent the stale, poisonous water from seeping into his mouth. He shot down through the inky, bitter depths, clawing through spears of water grass and long, clammy chains of frog eggs which resembled period marks on a celluloid ribbon. Muck, slime, sludge.

Then his legs were on the gluey bottom of the moat. His groping shins banged on the rough outlines of the box. His hands closed on the handles, and he struck out for the surface.

Heavy objects move easily under water. Seconds later, Deo Daley kicked his way to the top, through clinging green slime and a smudge of roiling, black mud as thick as syrup.

His head rummaged through the round, oily water pads which floated like disks of green varnish on the scummy water. Then Tex Garland's gnarled old claws helped him pull the streaming camphor-wood chest against the bank of rubberlike, oozing mud.

With feverish haste, the two men opened the bullet-perforated trunk, while Deo Daley clung to the wiry grass of the bank and kept the spouting box from sinking back into the depths.

Tex Garland hurled back the lid and peered into the trunk, which was filled with oily, sediment-swimming water. His moan of despair gave way to a shriek of bewilderment. The apples turned green on his cheeks.

Deo Daley released his grip on the bank and sloshed his arms to the elbows in the water-filled box, stirring them about as his flinching fingers sought for Irene's water-logged, yielding flesh.

But Irene was gone! The chest was empty. Empty save for the slushy water which squirted from a dozen bullet holes in its brown wooden sides. And the filthy moat held the grim secret of her disappearance!

When Irene Garland felt the trunk containing her body toppling over the brink of the Alcazar's lofty wall, a merciful faint spared her senses the ordeal of whizzing down through space.

The crushing impact of the dropping chest carried the trunk below the water, and the crash against the surface of the moat sprang gaping seams along all four corners of the ancient box.

Cold, evil-smelling water, gushing in through the cracks and the bullet holes, revived the girl as the chest bobbed to the top. In an instant, she saw that the box would not remain afloat more than a few fleeting seconds.

Gasping up the last lungful of air left in the trunk, Irene Garland struggled frantically as she felt the waters closing about her body. Then, with a final gurgle, the trunk filled and settled in a slow spiral to the bottom of the moat.

But the girl's hand had discovered one fact—the force of the fall had not only split the box panels, making it sink more speedily, but had also finished the job of breaking the brass lock, which Chirlo's bullet had damaged.

The trunk settled to a resting place on the bottom of the ancient moat, with its lid downward. The girl had only to lift her bruised and throbbing back to open the chest.

Out of the alligator mouth of the trunk's lid she crept, like a turtle leaving its sandy nest. Sour muck slushed about her as she crawled free of the chest that would have been her coffin of doom, and the trunk settled shut once more.

Irene's twenty years of outdoor living had taught her to think fast and true in emergencies. And now, with her lungs filled with staling air from which her body had already burned the oxygen, she knew that she must head for the surface at once.

But to do that, she realized, would be to expose her lucky escape to the leering outlaws who were doubtlessly leaning over the walls above, watching her death bubbles wriggling to the surface.

And if they captured her again, she realized her fate would be speedy, and far more gruesome. She had seen enough of the torture chamber of the *Alcazar de los Ladrones* to know that.

Magically, the picture of Deo Daley, bound with iron bands to the whipping post down in the dungeon, flashed through Irene's head. Irene commenced swimming along the bottom of the moat, until she had covered about ten yards from the spot where the trunk had settled.

Then, her bursting lungs forcing her to ascend, she followed the V-shaped banks of the moat upward. Her head slipped noiselessly out of the water. As she sucked great gasps of air into her throbbing lungs, she saw that she was in the midst of a great bed of lily pads which formed a sour crust along the moat's bank.

Quick as the movement of a toad, she lifted one of the umbrella-like pads and pulled it over her head. Thus protected from being seen from above, she stood for many minutes in the oozy sludge, while the glossy, waxen surface of the lily pad covered her head like a miniature parasol of green oilcloth.

Her fingers found and twisted off the stem of the pad. Holding it against her chest, Irene dived once more, this time swimming up the moat until her groping arms found the mossy logs of the ruined drawbridge which dammed the ditch.

Again she broke water, this time bearing with her the saucer-shaped lily pad, which shielded her from view while she treaded water and breathed, her head under the green, oily pad.

Risking possible discovery, the girl laid aside the floating lily pad and glanced about her. She saw no one on the wall above. Little did she dream that even while she had been in the act of swimming under water to that bridge, her father had crossed it!

Out of the gray water she climbed, like a soaked seal crawling out on a rock. Up the corrugated surface of the wrecked drawbridge she made her way, until she stood in safety on the threshold of the castle, her body absorbing the hot sun rays.

But she realized she must not wait there. Shivering with anxiety, she made her way to the door in the castle wall, and hid back in the shadows. Her heart turned to a chunk of ice as she heard footsteps slogging up the dungeon stairs and out the door.

In her mind, Irene pictured those two running figures as Don Chirlo and Curt Thode. But in reality, she had hidden while the scout of Terror Trail and her own father passed by, on their way to investigate the sunken trunk from which she had just escaped!

"Now I can save Deo!" thought the girl, satisfied in her own mind that the two men who had just bolted out of the castle wall were her enemies. "Then we can find guns and—"

Out of her shadowy niche the girl crept, making her way up to the corridor. Then she stood stock-still as there came to her alarmed ears the sound of padding footsteps and Curt Thode's voice inquiring: "Didn't you hear somebody runnin', Chirlo?"

Then the outlaw king's voice, sinister as a gun shot: "Bah! Daley no escaped, and the *muchacha* ees drown'."

Irene whirled to run, then screamed as she ran into the very arms of Curt Thode! Quick as light, the outlaw snapped out a six-gun and jammed it in the girl's ribs.

130

STALKING FIGHT

"THOSE ARE THE STEPS YOU HEARD, Thode!" chuckled Don Chirlo as he reached out like a striking snake to seize Irene Garland in his huge, gorilla-like arms. "She must be magic, to get out o' that box."

Thode's mustached upper lip curled off glittering white teeth as he lowered his cocked .45 and holstered it, seeing the girl safely captured.

"This time she won't get out of a busted box!" snarled Thode, in tones which turned Irene's arteries into strings of frost. "Come on, Chirlo! We'll take 'er down to the dungeon an' finish off both her an' Deo Daley tergether! They'll enjoy seein' each other squirm on those torture machines!"

"Go git a torch, Thode!" ordered Don Chirlo, taking a fresh grip on the girl, who now cowered, wet-faced, but with courage blazing in her blue eyes, in his grasp. "We'll take her down to the torture den, then we weel find her padre an' breeng heem." "

Anxious to get the business of torturing their victims under way, Curt Thode departed in search of a torch. Failing to find the one which Chirlo had left on the floor, he decided it had gone out during the interval, and continued his way to the castle. He returned with a blazing chunk of pine which he had found in the hearth.

Thus equipped, they once more descended into the hollow depths of the dungeon beneath the Alcazar, not stopping until they had reached the torture chamber, hewn out of the living bedrock.

The first thing that met their eyes was the empty, dangling rusty iron bands hanging from the oaken

131

frame of the whipping post.

"The scout o' Terror Trail has escaped!" gasped Don Chirlo.

A trill of joyous laughter burst from Irene's lips at the sight. She knew, now, the meaning of those other footsteps she had heard.

For a moment, the two outlaws were on the verge of panic as they were thus faced by the inexplicable escape of their second prisoner. A quick inspection of the torture machinery of the chamber convinced Curt Thode that their victim was not hiding inside the den, at any rate.

"That means he's gone out o' here!" grated Thode, returning with the torch to where Don Chirlo held their now smiling prisoner. "An' somebody helped him out o' those iron bands. It's a cinch—"

An oath sawed through Don Chirlo's mouth as he cranked his head about to peer at the steps behind them.

"The old padre, Tex Garland, heard the shots! He rescued the scout o' Terror Trail!" raged the outlaw, turning to carry Irene Garland to the whipping post. *"Andale!* Both them hombres ees lookin' for us, then. Eet was their footsteps we heard."

The two crooks handled their girl prisoner with rough and hasty hands as they clamped iron bands about her neck, arms, and ankles, even as they had imprisoned the scout of Terror Trail a short time before.

But now, the satisfaction of knowing that both her father and Deo Daley were alive made her not mind being left alone in this pit-black chamber of horror, surrounded by the grim implements of agony transplanted to this amazing castle from the historic

132

days of the Spanish Inquisition.

Thode took the precaution of tying a gag about the girl's mouth. Then, rocking her head on her shoulders with a contemptuous slap, he and Don Chirlo took the torch and bounded up the steps with drawn guns and alert eyes, to search for Daley and Garland.

On the moat bank outside, Deo Daley was just climbing out of the water, his fringed sleeves and leggings streaming water as he released his grip on the sieve-bottomed chest.

Tex Garland, his eyes blank with horror and grief, watched the box slide down out of sight into the mire of the moat bottom as if it were the casket of his daughter being lowered into a grave.

"She's—drowned! She's down there somewhere!" choked the old man piteously, clutching the scout's shoulder. "Dive again!"

Daley shook his head as he gathered up his six-gun belt and bandoleer and buckled them about him.

"I don't think she was in the box, Tex!" retorted the scout, panting. "That means she's in the castle, an' in danger. Thode an' Chirlo are in there. We've got to save her."

While Tex Garland wracked his brains at the possibility of the two outlaws having slipped by his sentinel post, the two men ran back to the castle gate and into the courtyard plaza.

"Here! They took my gun—give me your hogleg, an' you use your rifle!" commanded the scout, as they hurried down a dank, echo-filled hallway and ascended a flight of stairs which led them to the main lobby, or banquet hall, of the Castle of Thieves. "We'll dive here an' hunt every room till we find her!"

Both armed, Deo Daley and the missing girl's father parted company, each taking a side of the castle and searching for evidence of the outlaws they knew to be somewhere within the place.

Br-rang! A gun blast ripped the echoes minutes later, and Tex Garland went sprawling on his face, a slug plowing a red line along his scalp.

Bullet-dazed, he was too weak to hear or see the form of Curt Thode race out of the shadows behind him, a smoking six-gun in his palm, a triumphant gleam in his pit-black orbs.

"I got one of 'em, Chirlo!" yelled the traitor, turning Garland over and satisfying himself that the grazing shot had put the old pioneer out of the fight. "Watch out for that scout o' Terror Trail! He's prob'ly around somewhere's close!"

From somewhere back in the castle, a grunt told Curt Thode that the half-breed leader of the outlaw gang was stalking through shadowy hallways, searching for the young frontier scout.

Through a moldy and spider-webby curtain, Curt Thode shouldered his way to the edge of the castle lobby. Across the room, the dying fire in the massive hearth made a cloudy layer of smoke in the room, as the ancient clogged chimney did not draw well.

Gun close to his side, Thode's darting eyes searched for a glimpse of Deo Daley. But even as he took one step out on the floor, he heard a snarl of fury behind him, and he whirled.

Crack! A bullet knocked the weapon from Thode's hand.

Out of an arched doorway branching off from the lobby sprang the water-doused figure of the scout of Terror Trail, his sultry eyes gleaming as he advanced

134

on Curt Thode with a cocked .45.

"Grab a cloud pronto, Thode! An' if you get crimpy, I'll let you have it in the briskit!"

Curt Thode read grim death in the blackness of Daley's Colt muzzle. Back at Fort Adios, he had seen the scout's amazing skill with a six-gun, knew it would be useless to resist.

Daley came forward, his hands frisking Thode for another weapon. The trembling spy turned as Daley prodded him about with six-gun barrel and made a quick search for a possible hidden knife.

The air was blue with smoke, and Daley's eyes smarted. Perhaps that was why he did not notice the lurking figure of Don Chirlo slinking along the railed balcony just over their heads.

Now, moving with catlike stealth, the big outlaw straddled the stone railing of the balcony which rimmed the lobby, and posed like a diver not ten feet above Deo Daley's head.

"Now get goin', Thode!" ordered the scout briskly. "I'll—"

Crash! Like a ton of bricks, the black-clad bulk of Don Chirlo hurtled down out of the air to knock Deo Daley floorward.

A shower of stars exploded in the scout's skull. He fought against unconsciousness as he felt Chirlo's iron hands seize him. Then the six-gun was jerked from his fingers by Curt Thode.

Before the scout of Terror Trail could recover from the shock of his unexpected attack, Don Chirlo had unbuckled the cartridge-studded bandoleer which crossed Daley's chest and used it to bind the scout's arms tightly to his sides.

"Well, we got the three of 'em at last!" panted Curt

Thode, rubbing sweat off his swarthy face. "An' you've escaped us for the last time, Daley. We ain't takin' no more risks. Inside o' half an hour you're hittin' the greased skids to hell!"

Daley returned Don Chirlo's level stare, determined that the scar-faced outlaw should not read the despair which was forming in his heart, curdling his veins.

"You might at least tell me what you did with the girl!" grated the scout of Terror Trail through tight lips. "One thing, even with us dead, you won't get any gold out o' this castle."

Don Chirlo shrugged and laid a rough hand on Daley's fringed buckskin sleeve.

"As for the *oro*—eet ees enough reward to have found thees castle. Eet weel make a wonderful hideout," retorted the outlaw, apparently not disappointed on hearing again that the gold he had hoped to find did not exist. "An' as for the girl—*caramba!* You shall see her ver' soon, *si!* Ver' soon indeed!"

Thode, who had ducked through the curtains a moment before, returned with the stunned body of Tex Garland jackknifed over one shoulder. Daley, who realized that their doom had come at last, felt actual regret upon seeing that Thode's bullet had not finished off the old man. If it had, he would have escaped the tortures that were no doubt facing him when he returned to consciousness.

There followed the grueling nightmare of once more going down the haunted steps of the dungeon, where Don Picadero had installed his devilish machines of torture. It would be the last time they went down them alive, of that Deo Daley was certain.

The doom chamber looked twice as ghostly and

gruesome now under the wavering pink light of the smoky torches which Thode and Chirlo installed in wall niches.

Old man Garland was coming to his senses slowly, but he had been disarmed, and Thode laid his body out on the stone floor in front of the whipping post where Irene Garland, gagged, stood staring at Deo Daley, her eyes flooded with horror.

"Don't worry any, Irene!" called out Daley, knowing the uselessness of trying to give any courage to the girl when their fates were hopeless. "We'll all three of us be over the Big Divide before long, out o' reach o' devils like Thode an' Chirlo. An' we can be happy, at least, that they won't get the gold they came after!"

Tears traced twin streams down Irene's cheeks and under the bandanna gag as she saw Don Chirlo spank his palms together, grin broadly, and look about him, as if selecting which of the numerous engines of torture he would employ first.

"Ah, a torture furnace!" chuckled the outlaw, his eyes lighting on a fireplace affair whose open chimney was fitted with iron bands similar to those on the whipping post which held Irene Garland.

"Here, Daley, ees where Don Picadero burned hees victims alive. An' that"—he paused to enjoy the looks of horror which grew in the faces of Daley and Irene—"weel be the padre's fate."

Irene made throttled noises with her throat as Tex Garland's dazed body was jerked up to his feet by Don Chirlo and brought over to the furnace used for human torture.

Deo Daley was struggling with the strap which bound his arms. He could not afford to make a bolt

137

yet, for Curt Thode held him in check with a cocked .45 leveled at his abdomen.

The torture furnace was little more than a fireplace, on the back stones of which were straps for holding the victim. The top of the chimney led off through the stone ceiling. Fires would be built at the victim's feet, and soon the draft would bring the flames upward, enveloping the body like a living candle.

Such was the fate Chirlo had selected for Tex Garland.

Deo Daley, aware of the leveled six-gun in Thode's hands, struggled helplessly with his bonds as he saw Don Chirlo lift old man Garland's body up into the fireplace chimney and clang shut the rusted iron bands about his neck, arms, and ankles.

Next Chirlo proceeded to shatter an ancient chair against a wall until it was a mass of pith-dry kindling wood. These fragments he placed in a heap below Tex Garland's booted foot. And at that moment, Irene Garland slumped into a faint of horror.

With his hands already grasping a blazing torch with which to ignite the old pioneer's fire of death, Chirlo noticed that Irene was insensible. The big half-breed turned to Daley and Thode with a booming laugh, fierce as a lion's roar in the torture den.

"Hah! We shall wait for the girl to see her padre squirming een the flames," snarled the big outlaw, replacing the torch in its wall niche. "An' while we wait, we shall see what weel be the fate of our frien', the scout of Terror Trail!"

The outlaw was not long in discovering the instrument of agony he would use in destroying the life of his enemy. He walked into the shadows until he came to a circular pit, hewn out of the solid bedrock which floored the chamber.

A rumbling laugh, fierce as a panther's scream, issued from Chirlo's cavernous throat as he stood on the rim of the well and peered into its shuddery depths.

It was the famous "pit of spikes," first used during the days of the Spanish Inquisition. It was ten feet wide and eight feet deep, with its stone floor bored full of holes like a colander.

In each of these holes, which were spaced four inches apart, was fitted a spike of steel, sharp as a needle, and a half inch in thickness. The top of this bed of spikes was fifteen inches off the actual floor in which they were embedded in socket holes.

Even as Chirlo peered down into the ghastly pit of doom, he could see by the guttering rays of the torches that Don Picadero, three centuries before, had also cast a victim into that awful, spike-floored cistern.

Draped among the bristling, sharp-pointed steel rods was a human skeleton. The skull was pierced by one spike. Others sprouted through the ribs, two splintered a hip bone. It was like impaling a grasshopper on the points of a wire brush.

Chirlo turned about, booming with vicious triumph. And as he did so, he spied something else—perhaps the most famous device of ancient torture known to the world—an "Iron Maiden"!

It was a shell of iron, hinged like a door to the wall, and rusted the shade of orange peel by the dampness of the ages. It was shaped like a tenpin sawed down the middle. From the floor to the round knob of its top, the Iron Maiden was six feet high. Roughly, it might resemble the form of a human body.

Stepping forward, Don Chirlo seized a rusty iron

handle and swung the doorlike shell of iron outward, to expose a similar-shaped cavity, like the bottom piece of a mummy case, hollowed out of the stone wall and backed with yellow-painted oaken planks.

The interior side of the iron door was studded with sharp-pointed rods similar to the bottom of the pit of spikes. When a victim was placed against the yellow planks and the iron door shut upon him, he would thus be pinned to the wooden wall in a score of places. In the Middle Ages, the Iron Maiden had claimed untold hundreds of unfortunate wretches who had incurred the wrath of kings.

"Deo Daley shall go into the pit of spikes!" decreed Don Chirlo, turning away from the Iron Maiden. "An' the girl, *she* shall die inside thees Iron Maiden!"

For a moment, sanity reeled inside Deo Daley's brain. His tugging arms drew strength from his desperation and slipped a bit in his bandoleer-strap bonds. But Curt Thode, noticing the fact, merely grinned. He would cripple Daley with a bullet if he managed to free himself. It would be a pleasant duty, maiming him.

Tex Garland now had recovered consciousness, and a bellow of rage and horror burst through his beard as he saw Don Chirlo grab the body of his daughter, Irene, who was now also awakened.

"Chirlo! Hands off that girl, you demon! I'll kill you with my bare hands if you—"

Sweat rained off Daley's face as he wrenched furiously on his bonds, unheedful of the gun barrel which Curt Thode held in readiness. His veins ran cold as he saw Don Chirlo, with rapid movements, release the girl from her steel bonds and drag her, kicking and struggling, toward the grim, red-rusted Iron Maiden.

The cold walls of the torture chamber rang with mocking cries of anguish and helpless rage as the two men saw Don Chirlo pull open the door of the Iron Maiden and, with a brutal surge of power, push Irene Garland back against the yellow plank wall inside the tenpin-shaped cavity, where she would stand when the tearing, rending spikes of the Iron Maiden's metal cover closed upon her.

Tex Garland writhed like a lizard with a crushed spine, but he was bolted flat against the chimney of the torture furnace, his toes inches from a heap of sticks which would be ignited to cook him to a crisp. In his eagerness to kill Irene, Chirlo apparently was going to spare her the agony of seeing her father burn.

Curt Thode, grinning like a devil's mask, stood behind Deo Daley and watched the scout clawing his arms inch by inch from his bonds, scraping skin and flesh as he did so. The instant he was free, Thode planned to smash Daley's knee with a .45 slug.

Now Don Chirlo was stepping back, as the girl remained paralyzed with speechless horror inside the Iron Maiden's wall cavity. The big outlaw's hands grabbed the hinged iron door, the inside of which bristled with the ugly, death-dealing spikes.

Slowly, he began to swing it forward in the girl's gag-bound face. Only her eyes moved, following that swinging iron door as it swung closer and closer to her body.

Though his arms were not yet free, Deo Daley could stand it no longer. Bawling a scream of desperation, he leaped forward. But Curt Thode reached out a boot to trip him, and he crashed heavily on his face.

Daley got to his knees with hammers beating his temples and his vision blurring. Then he realized that even if his hands were free, he would be too late to span the space between himself and Irene.

With a snarl of triumph, Don Chirlo clanged the door of the Iron Maiden completely shut upon the horror-stiffened figure of Irene Garland!

SPIKED DEATH

THE SILENCE WAS as thick as if it had turned to marble. Even the treacherous Curt Thode could not restrain a shudder of horror as the iron door crunched shut with a grisly thud against its socket outside the sulphur-yellow planks.

Tex Garland's eyes glazed with the horror which only a father could feel at his daughter's murder. He ceased his hoarse cries of hate. The thudding of the door stopped his pitiful begging. He became a thing of wood as he hung there, suspended in the torture-furnace fireplace. Doom could not come too quickly to him, now—

And even Don Chirlo, most vicious of all frontier outlaws, turned a shade paler as he started to back slowly away from the iron shell, staring at the Iron Maiden with bulging eyes, creeping back from the grim machine of death as if he feared the ghost of his victim might strike his evil heart with lightning.

"I'll kill you both!" Harsh as the snarl of a wild beast, the sound yanked through Deo Daley's throat as he jerked his hands free at last from the strap which held them down.

The scout of Terror Trail was almost insane with rage, a human cyclone of vengeance. Whirling, he charged at Curt Thode, his eyes blazing like twin red

142

fires.

Curt Thode still gripped his .45, but he had not expected the young scout to turn and attack him first. He had believed Daley would spring at Don Chirlo. Thode had even swung his gun barrel about to trigger a bullet through Daley's legs if he made such a move.

The scout's fist caught Thode over the heart, and all went black for the treacherous spy before Thode's stunned brain could telegraph a message to tense his trigger finger.

Down like a sack of meat slumped Curt Thode. Before he hit the floor, Deo Daley had jerked the crook's six-gun from Thode's fingers and was whirling, his face red with hate.

Don Chirlo, backing away from the Iron Maiden, turned and jelled into a statue of ice as he saw the scout of Terror Trail bring the long-barreled Colt up. Slow, deliberate, cold as snow, Deo Daley was leveling the 45 straight between the crook's eyes.

The bandit leader knew he could expect no mercy. There was no time to draw his own holstered gun. He winced as all time seemed to stand still, and waited for Daley to fire point-blank.

Clack! The scout groaned as he heard the firing pin fall on an empty chamber.

And before he could spin the cylinder again, he saw Don Chirlo glide into action. Chirlo's own .45 leaped from its leather, swung up.

Br-rang! Chirlo's gun roared like a cannon in the torture chamber.

But the bullet zipped over Daley's shoulder and tore coals from a flickering torch in the wall niche behind the scout as Daley dropped to a crouch. At the same instant, he hurled his useless gun like a thunderbolt, straight at Chirlo's blazing ˙45.

Clang! Daley's flying gun split Chirlo's thumb as it smacked the bucking Colt from the outlaw's grasp. Following that hurtling gun like a bullet came Deo Daley, his face a horrid mask questing for revenge, fists knotted into killing chunks of knuckle.

Again, in a split clock tick, Chirlo saw death coming toward him. He knew there would be no time to grope back in the shadows for his fallen six-gun. It was showdown now, with fist and brawn.

Chirlo stiffened, braced himself to meet the scout's flailing charge. Again Don Chirlo became the leering self-confident killer, sure of his own tremendous physical strength.

Crack! Thud! Ribs split as the two men came together like colliding trains.

Chirlo's head bobbed on his shoulders like a punching bag on a rack. Chirlo had the advantage of weight, but he had not reckoned on fighting a tornado, a kicking horse, a stick of dynamite, and a wildcat rolled into one package.

The look of despair cleared in Tex Garland's eyes as he hung helpless in his steel bonds over the pile of matchwood intended for his own funeral pyre. He forgot that the door of the Iron Maiden had clanged shut on his daughter only seconds before.

New hope throbbed in the old man's veins as he witnessed the most amazing battle of all time, between two hate-festered, savage men. And was there ever a more ghastly background for a tearing, punching, rough-and-tumble battle between mighty enemies?

A torture room chiseled out of bedrock. Far below the foundations of a rotting Spanish castle. A torture den filled with racks and gallows, guillotines and spiked pits, an Iron Maiden, and a furnace where humans were broiled alive.

Out in the center of the floor they were, locked in a grapple which could only end in the death of one or both. A man huge as a bull gorilla, powerful as a crazy elephant, hard as rocks, and heartless as a stone image. Matched against a wiry, lean, desperate young frontier scout, whippy as a cougar, his fists powered with a rage for revenge which was not to be denied.

The flickering light of the torches danced off the sweat which oozed from the pores of the men as they bruised to the floor and rolled over each other. Punching and twisting, pummeling and breaking, gone mad with the fury of lightning-swift combat.

It was a fray between Deo Daley, frontier trail scout, who represented all that was lawful and honest in a wild, untamed country infested with evil and crawling with human vermin, and Don Chirlo, the scar-faced leader of a gang that had been a scourge of the border frontier for countless seasons.

Breaking, they stood knee against knee and slugged. Deo Daley, swept off his footing by the fury of Chirlo's rush, fell back against a torture rack, and it showered into matchwood. Only the fact that the outlaw stumbled over the stirring body of Curt Thode saved Daley from having fatal fingers clamp over his throat.

But before Chirlo could get to his feet again, Daley was dancing away, shaking his head to clear his brain from the effect of his crash. His battered muscles and shocked spine throbbed.

Again they met, with a thudding jar of fists. Chirlo was fighting foul, with clawing nails and snapping teeth and kicking boots. Daley, tiring, had become

145

steadier, cooler, fighting with a grim, dogged speed which dazzled Tex Garland as he watched the fight sweeping to its grim climax, chill with the promise of death.

Timing his punches, hopping on feet as light as the four winds, the scout of Terror Trail was punishing Chirlo's black-clad body with skin-smashing blows in what he knew was his last spurt of offensive. Then they swung about, sparred momentarily like boxers in a ring, changing positions, hunting for an opening.

Then Deo Daley got a glimpse of the Iron Maiden in the background.

The sight fired his veins to the boiling point. His jaded muscles writhed under his skin, knotted with fresh, driving power. He had been in the act of dropping into a defensive battle, but now he carried an unexpected rush into Chirlo's very arms.

Wham! Sock! For the first time since the amazing spectacle of hand-to-hand slaughter had begun, Don Chirlo was forced to cover up and retreat, trying to claw into a clinch.

But he found the rain of punches increasing. Snarling in his throat like a wounded grizzly, the scout of Terror Trail was driving at Chirlo with head lowered and teeth grated, brown hair tumbling in a screen over his bloodshot eyes, blood pouring from a score of bruises and tears and cuts.

Spat! Even Tex Garland's grief-dulled ears caught the sound of Daley's final supreme uppercut smacking home on the outlaw king's jaw.

Chirlo's head snapped backward, exposing a stubbly throat. He staggered backward on the smooth stone floor. Then Don Chirlo felt his heels drop into nothingness, found his boot soles tottering on the circular rim of a hole.

With a squeal of desperate fear, Don Chirlo thrashed his arms like windmills and jackknifed his body forward as he fought for balance on the side of the well of death into which he had intended to throw the scout.

Don Chirlo collapsed, and plunged backward with a yell of frenzy. He landed with a grisly, ripping sound upon the needle-bristling floor of the pit of spikes!

The scout of Terror Trail pitched ahead two steps, slumped to his knees, and fell on all fours at the brink of the pit.

He looked down. Don Chirlo's mighty body was there, writhing like some queer black bug in its death throes. Stretched out on those rusty spikes beside the skeleton of a victim of Don Picadero's. But he was not suffering. A spike had driven like a nail through one temple, bringing instant, merciful death to Don Chirlo the scar-faced.

The bandit's legs quivered and were still, lying on the forest of sharpened iron rods. The silver spangles of his bell-bottomed *gaucho* trousers chimed against the iron, went silent. Blossoms of blood spread on Chirlo's white silk girdle.

The career of the frontier's worst criminal was ended. But strangely, Dec, Daley did not feel a thrill of triumph as he got to his feet and stood there, shoulders humped, body dripping wet and shining with blood. Even if Irene's doom was avenged, it did not bring her back. And suddenly Deo Daley found that she meant more to him than all the world combined.

Curt Thode, the treacherous, slinking spy of the dead outlaw's band, pulled himself to his feet, felt himself for a gun, then backed off into the shadows as he saw Daley turning slowly, a battered wreck of a man.

Crawling sidewise like a crab, glistening eyes watching the young scout, Curt Thode finally turned and fled into the darkness, to escape the wrath of the man who had killed Don Chirlo.

"You—you did nobly, son!" whispered Tex Garland as Deo Daley went with dragging steps to release the whiskered old veteran from the fireplace.

"I—I almost feel like I don't want to live any more," was Deo Daley's soundless answer. "I—it seems—"

And then, for the first time, the scout of Terror Trail observed the fact that Curt Thode had made his escape. A flush mounted Daley's fist-battered face, and he turned to Tex Garland with a snarl of hate.

"My job isn't finished, Tex!" snapped the young plainsman, his voice awful to hear. "That snake, Curt Thode, is even lower than Don Chirlo. Thode betrayed his flag at Fort Adios. He spied on his friends. I'm goin' to kill that rat with my bare hands. Come on, Tex!"

The old man's eyes went wet as he shook his head. "Revenge belong to youth, son," whispered the old Texan slowly. "I—I reckon—while you're runnin' down Thode—I'll stay up here—to be with Irene."

Daley sobered, his eyes boring into Garland's. Neither of them wanted to look over there on the wall, where the Iron Maiden was.

Just then something reached their ears. Something that made them snap their exhausted bodies rigid. A voice! A whisper from yesterday, calling to them out of the stillness that packed that den of death and torture and agony and doom:

"Daddy! Deo!"

Cold sweat sprinkled Daley's face. Tex Garland swayed, a little sick. There was no mistaking that voice. It was Irene!

Were they going crazy? Had the ordeal they had just escaped sapped the reason from their minds?

Deo Daley, like a stiff-jointed doll coming to life, broke the chains which held his paralyzed muscles. With a cry, he bolted across the floor, to stand in front of the rusty Iron Maiden. His fingers spread out like the roots of a brush; his chest rose and fell.

Again that voice, issuing like a muffled whisper through the rust-speckled hinges of that Iron Maiden shell:

"Daddy! Deo!"

Tex Garland stole to Daley's side. Sweat trickled down the scout's face, collected in a pearly drop on his jaw. Then the scout's fingers stole forward inch by inch, to coil damply about the iron handle of the Iron Maiden's case. Both knew that those spikes were long enough to go through the girl's body like pins.

It was inconceivable that she cquld still be alive. It would be a sight to haunt their dreams through eternity, when they opened that door. Yet they knew they must do it.

Breathing a prayer, the scout of Terror Trail tugged the Iron Maiden gently open. His body winced as he expected the mangled body of the girl he loved to fall into his arms in death.

"Deo! Daddy! Oh-h-h-h—you've come!"

A pair of doeskin-sleeved arms shot out of the Iron Maiden's interior to clasp about their necks. Irene Garland, her body untorn and unpierced by the bristling spikes, was clinging to her deliverers, as uninjured as if this had all been a weird nightmare!

"You're alive!" Daley's sputtering ceased as he held Irene at arm's length and saw that she was indeed unscathed.

Then his incredible gaze turned to look at the Iron Maiden, and there he saw the climax which fate had reserved for them.

The oak-planked, lemon-yellow back of the Iron Maiden's socket had swung back on grass-green corroded-brass hinges. It exposed a doorway to a chamber that was as black as a hod of soot.

It was a full five minutes before the father and lover turned from the girl who had been literally restored from another world, to determine the amazing prank of fate which had spared her from a torture device that had never before spared a victim.

"As soon as Chirlo stood me against the plank back of that cavity," explained Irene breathlessly, "I could feel the yellow planks yield, as if I were leaning against an open door.

"As he closed the spiked door, I cringed back—and fell flat on my back into a dark room. As soon as I could get my gag off my mouth I started screaming. But I thought you were both dead."

With a yell, Deo Daley ran across the room and jerked down one of the blazing torches from its wall niche. Holding it aloft, he ran to the Iron Maiden, opened the ten-pin-shaped door wider, and held the firebrand into the mysterious room which had lain hidden behind the yellow-colored oaken door of the Iron Maiden.

The fire shed its ruddy ray through darkness that had been undisturbed for a span of three centuries. The

150

stench of stale air which had been pocketed inside this chisel-hewn room in the solid bedrock assaulted his nostrils as the scout of Terror Trail adjusted his eyes and peered into the chamber of mystery.

What he saw staggered his vision. He was looking into a tiny cellar of a room, which was tiered on either side of the opening with shelves, which in turn were laden with objects which glittered in the light, as if shrinking from this sudden intrusion.

"Tex! Irene! This Iron Maiden formed the door to Picadero's treasure vault!" exclaimed Daley. "We've found the secret of the Castle of Thieves at last! That gold really existed, after all!"

They were right. Ingots of yellow metal were tiered like cordwood on the shelves. Molded and rotting leather pokes had broken to spill out a shower of tarnished disks-doubloons and guineas, golden coins of the Middle Ages.

Jewels shed spears of liquid fire in the flare of the torch—purple and red, yellow and white, blue and green. Sparkling, eye-dazzling ropes of precious stones, cameos, silver rings, gem-encrusted brooches. The booty of a hundred pirate raids of long ago!

They had found the store vault of the plunder of Don Picadero, the treasure loot of an ancient Spanish buccaneer.

PIRATE PLUNDER

DEO DALEY DOUBTED HIS OWN EYES, even as he eld aloft his torch of flaming pinewood, and watched the flickering light dissolve the darkness of the stuffy chamber.

151

"It's all ours, Irene—Spanish treasure!" breathed the frontier scout, tightening his buckskin-clad arm about the wide-eyed girl who stood at his side. "We've risked our lives to get it, but now that we've found it, we're rich as kings, all of us!"

Rich as twenty kings! The vault was small, but its walls were lined with shelves, and each shelf was sagging with the booty of a hundred buccaneer raids of long ago.

Ingots of yellow gold formed little log houses on the rock floor. Fusty leather bags, rotten with time, brittle as paper, had broken to disgorge pyramids of tarnished golden disks along the shelves.

Irene Garland stepped forward into the pit. She knelt and ran her bronzed fingers through a stack of the coins, staring at the odd, crowned heads which were stamped on the money.

"It—it don't seem possible, does it, son?" whispered Tex Garland, his eyes twinkling in the ruddy rays of Daley's pine-knot torch. "Seems like we're dreamin'. This whole treasure hunt o' ourn has been unreal, from start to finish."

The scout of Terror Trail watched Irene get to her feet, letting the last of the gold coins slide through her hands. His eyes focused on the boxes of jewels, sacks of coins, piles of solid gold bullion. Rubies twinkled like red warning lights, and, strange to say, they did awaken a warning of danger in Daley's mind.

"While I've been feastin' my eyes on this gold, I plumb forgot that that spy, Curt Thode, is escapin' out o' this castle" exclaimed the scout, turning to Tex Garland and Irene. "You two stay here an' play with this treasure, an' I'll go out an' gun that rat down before he joins Don Chirlo's crooks outside."

Out into another chamber, Deo Daley made his way. He paused only long enough to take a second flaming torch from a wall niche. He did not care to inspect the weird engines of Spanish torture which filled that dungeon keep under the ancient Castles of Thieves.

"I'll catch Thode before he gets to the river!" swore Daley, stopping to pick up a six-gun from the floor. Up a steep flight of steps Daley made his way, the torch shedding red rays against the dank, mossy walls.

The flames so close to his hard-set, determined face contracted the pupils of his eyes. That was why, as he strode on noiseless moccasins up the stairs, Deo Daley did not notice a shadow detach itself from a gloom-packed corner behind him.

The scout of Terror Trail heard a rush of wind. He spun about, in time to see the barrel of a six-gun club descending above his very skull. His startled eyes saw a leering, evil face, set with black eyes and snarling white teeth.

Then the steel barrel thudded home against his scalp, and Deo Daley slumped to his knees. Showers of fireworks exploded in his head. Then all went black.

Curt Thode carefully hostered the six-gun with which he had clubbed the young scout's skull, and yanked a bandanna from a pocket to mop sweat off his glistening face.

The spy had witnessed, only a few minutes before, the struggle in which Deo Daley had slain his leader, Don Chirlo. Thode had thought to flee from that castle of doom. But as he hid back in the shadows, waiting for a safe opportunity to hurry out of the torture den, he had seen them make their astonishing discovery of the secret door of the pirate treasure vault. Thode was

153

as cowardly as a coyote, but his greed for gold triumphed.

He had remained hidden in the darkness, intending to wait until his enemies had left the dungeon. Then he could seize a sack of gold for himself, wait for the coming of night, and escape from the *Alcazar de los Ladrones* unseen by Deo or his party.

"I reckon I killed the salty young sprout without rousin' the attention o' Garland or the gal," panted Thode to himself, as he stood over Deo Daley's inert form. "They couldn't a heard me."

The guttering torch had subsided to a club of pink coals. Curt Thode scrubbed the last bit of glow from the firebrand with one boot sole, then stooped and picked up Deo Daley's body.

Up the dark stairs he staggered with his unconscious burden. He could not afford to have Tex Garland or Irene discover Daley's body on the steps. Then they would know Thode was still around, and would guard themselves accordingly. And both were crack shots.

An evil plot was forming in Curt Thode's poisonous brain, as he plodded silently up the ancient steps leading out of the dungeon. Why not bring Don Chirlo's killer gang in there to slay Tex and Irene Garland?

Reaching the top landing of the stairway, Curt Thode could dimly see the granite block walls, dank and clammy to the touch, surrounding him. Off to right or left extended the black tunnel of a corridor.

Dim, ghostly light leaked into the murk from some nearby opening. It glinted off the copper-bound corners of a coffin-like chest which stood, like an oldfashioned grandfather's clock, against one wall of the stair landing.

Thode lowered the scout's insensible body to the floor, made his way to the clocklike case and opened it. As he did so, a jangling pile of junk toppled out over him, making him spring back with a squall of fright.

Then, as his eyes became accustomed to the gloom, he saw that he had merely opened an old armor closet. The clanking metal which had tumbled out upon him was in reality a suit of Spanish armor. It now lay scattered about like the contents of an upset tinware wagon—a silver-plated helmet, heavy chain-mail coat, shin plates.

An evil leer lighted Thode's swart features. "Hm-m-m! A nice coffin for Daley—an' if this noise makes ol' Tex Garlyand proddy, he won't find no trace o' the scout o' Terror Trail."

So saying, Curt Thode picked up Daley's body and lugged it with difficulty to the open door of the armor box. Stepping high so as not to make further noise against the spilled armor pieces on the floor, Thode carefully propped Daley's slumped figure inside the coffinlike box, and swung the door shut on squeaky hinges.

Cramming the door closed, he found a hasp with a metal pin attached, which he quickly put in place.

Moving as quickly as possible without starting a series of betraying echoes, Curt Thode skulked his way to an open, round-arched doorway through which soft daylight streamed. He hurried down the steps, to merge in the grass-grown courtyard of the Castle of Thieves.

"Soon's I show up without Chirlo, they'll make me the leader o' their gang, I reckon!" chuckled the spy, as he headed out of the castle gate, leaped a wrecked log bridge which spanned a sour ditch forming the castle's moat, and headed out across the meadow in the center of which the Alcazar had been erected, many centuries before. "Especially when I uncrate Daley's corpse an' show 'em—"

Thode reached the foot of the cliffs, and stood before the mouth of the tunnel which led into the rock wall. Through the tunnel flowed the Rio Torcido; and that tunnel formed the only exit from the castle basin. At the far end, Don Chirlo's gang would be assembled, waiting for him.

The spy peeled off his shirt and jerked feet from boots, to dive into the gentle current of the Rio Torcido with a creamy splash.

Five minutes later, he was pulling himself out on the bank of the river on the other side of the cliff, to greet the anxious members of Don Chirlo's gang of crooks.

TRAPDOOR DANGER!

IRENE GARLAND laid down a rope of glittering diamonds, which she had held looped about her neck. Her aged father removed a corncob pipe from his gray beard, scratched an apple-hued cheek with the chewed stem.

"All the diamonds an' rubies an' pearls in the whole world couldn't make you any more beautiful than you already are, Irene!" he said, holding up the guttering torch to inspect his daughter, there in the confines of Picadero's plunder vault. "You're a real queen, fit for any castle."

"I—I'm worried about Deo, Daddy," said the girl,

putting the diamonds aside. "Let's get out of here—the treasure can wait. I want to see what's keeping him. He's been gone half an hour."

Tex Garland followed his daughter out of the treasure chamber, bearing the torch which dispelled the gloomy shadows.

"You don't have to get nervous about the scout o' Terror Trail, I reckon!" chuckled the old man. "He's prob'ly on his way back now, cleanin' his gun after killin' Curt Thode. "

Irene picked a pair of six-guns off the floor, looked to their cylinders, and gave her father one of them.

Father and daughter made their way outside the castle, went across the courtyard, and headed for the great portals of the castle walls—walls which surrounded the Alcazar itself like a square fence set around a stone box.

"I hear voices talkin'!" exclaimed the old man excitedly. "That means Daley captured Thode alive an' is bringin' him back."

The old man broke off, his jaw sagging. The two had just reached the gateway of the castle, and were looking out across the grassy saucer of meadow which floored that pit in the cliffs. And what they saw jelled their hearts into cold stone.

Trooping like an army across the gentle, rolling knolls, came almost forty armed men, headed by Curt Thode!

Irene's eyes widened, and she raised a hand to her lips in terror as she saw the weltering sun rays gleaming off half-naked Apaches, faces daubed with war paint and feathered war bonnets trailing from their heads.

Tex Garland saw bearded American outlaws,

carrying Winchester rifles and six-guns, stalking through the grass toward the castle. He saw sombreroed Mexicans, hips freighted with knives and .45s.

"Thode's brought back Don Chirlo's gang!" squawked Tex Garland, his face gray under the beard. "Then where—where's Daley?"

At the sound of Garland's startled cry, weird echoes relayed the words to the foremost of the oncoming outlaws, two hundred yards away. And like a charging army, they broke into a run, straight for the gates of the castle.

"Ain't no time to wonder what's become o' Daley!" roared the old Texan, seizing Irene's arm. "Quick, daughter—you run into the banquet hall o' the castle an' get all them guns we raked together. I left my rifle up on the castle wall yesterday—maybe with it an' my six-gun I can stand them crooks off until you get back."

Irene headed for the castle at a run. Her first shock of horror was over, and she was cool as ice, ready for the desperate emergency. Their only chance now was to keep Thode's outlaws from getting inside the castle walls.

Tex Garland sprinted into a doorway which pierced the wall, and rocketed up a set of stairs leading to a turret, where he had left a rifle the day before.

Running to a loophole which opened out over the moat, Garland pawed the sticky gray cobwebs aside, fanned away the pluming dust, and peered down upon the wrecked remains of a rotten drawbridge.

The yelling outlaws had assembled on the bank, as they picked their way cautiously across the sodden logs. A cackle of joy burst from Tex Garland's lips as he saw the drawbridge collapse completely, to leave the surface of the sour-smelling moat dotted with swimming heads. Then Garland. saw, with narrowing eyes, that Curt Thode had succeeded in getting across the moat and was now scrambling for the gate of the Alcazar.

Garland jerked out his six-gun, shoved it through the loophole, and thumbed bullets downward. Thode was already at the gate, out of range of Garland's .45, but the streaking bullets cut down, one by one, five outlaws who were poised on the outside bank getting ready to dive into the moat.

Their bodies splashed into the water, and the return fire of the outlaws at the loophole above merely ripped the powder smoke which drifted from the slotlike window. Tex Garland was inside, reloading.

Glancing bullets threw rock dust in the old man's face as he sprinted for the inner rail of the balcony. "Thode, you dirty devil!" The cry grated through Garland's beard as he brought up his hot six-gun to fire at the darting figure of Curt Thode, who was zigzagging across the courtyard below.

But Garland was too late. Thode had taken advantage of the precious seconds while the old man on the balcony above was reloading. Garland's fast-triggered shots chased the lieutenant up the castle steps. Then Thode had vanished inside the castle.

"You'll taste some hot lead from Irene's guns, fella!" ripped out the old veteran, as he leaped back to his loophole post to resume his desperate attempt to keep back the outlaws who were swimming the moat.

Irene Garland, her arms loaded with six-guns and .30-.30 rifles, brushed her way through the moldy curtains of the doorway leading out of the lobby room of the Alcazar.

Gun shots thundered from outside, where her father was standing off the outlaws below. But if she did not get the guns to him before his ammunition supply belt was emptied, all would be lost and the outlaws would be swarming inside the courtyard.

Panting heavily, she headed for the hallway leading outside the castle. But as she did so, she recoiled in alarm as she saw the lithe form of Curt Thode charge up the steps and into the corridor.

A savage yell burst from the spy's lips as he saw the girl up the hallway. Her arms were laden with weapons, and he knew she could not beat his lightning-swift draw.

Irene saw her danger in the same instant. As quick as the dart of a spider, she ducked into the doorway of a room at her elbow.

Brrang! Thode's bullets whined past her shoulder as she backed into the room and prepared to lay down her guns in order to seize one. Then she could fight Thode on his own terms.

But the girl did not have a chance to lay down the weapons which clogged her arms. For as she stepped back into a corner of the dark room, she felt the great slab of stone flooring under her feet suddenly drop out from under her.

With a scream of terror, Irene Garland plunged through the hidden trapdoor and fell into sickening black space . . .

Consciousness had returned slowly to Deo Daley, inside his stifling box prison. The back of his skull ached as if a bullet had nicked the bone. His whole body throbbed with pain. Colored sparks twinkled against the black rim of his senses.

Many minutes had passed after he opened his eyes,

before he was able to figure out his fate, collect his scattered wits, and try to remember.

Yes, he had been striding up the dungeon steps. Then—he remembered it now—the leering face of Curt Thode had appeared out of the shadows. Then all had gone blank.

"But where in hell has he cached me?" gasped the scout of Terror Trail, his eyes opened wide but no whit of daylight being visible. "Maybe the rat buried me alive."

Then Daley became aware of the fact that he was jammed, upright, into a cratelike box—a box so narrow it did not permit him to slump into a squatting position. His groping hands touched wooden panels not five inches in front of his nose.

Bam! Thud! Daley pounded the wooden door of the armor closet with knotted fists, as a wave of panic shot over him at the thought of being buried alive. The blows told him one thing: that the panels were of thick wood, and tightly locked outside.

Beady sweat burst out over his body as he twisted about inside the coffinlike prison. Already he was feeling groggy from lack of air. Another half hour, and he would suffocate.

The armor wardrobe wabbled on its base. It teetered against the stone wall of the stair landing, as the frantic scout inside twisted his body, and pounded the sides and back of the closet, hunting desperately for an opening.

And then, as Deo Daley attempted to crash through the locked door of the armor case with one shoulder, the tall crate teetered on the front edge of its base.

A yell burst from the scout's lips as he felt the box going off balance. What if it were poised on the brink of a wall, or over a yawning grave? Perhaps Curt Thode was standing outside, watching, gloating.

It was too late to regain balance. With a swishing of air, the armor closet pitched forward. Metal clanged as the box hit the scattered armor strewn about the landing on the floor.

For an instant, the box balanced over the silver helmet which lay among the chain mail and breast-plates. At the same moment, Deo Daley twisted his stunned body inside the crate, attempting to get over on his back.

The combined motions served to twist the coffin-shaped box over the brink of the stairs. With the weight of the scout of Terror Trail inside, the box continued down the steps, rolling over and over like a square beam banging down a roof.

Slam! Crash! Bam! The castle's stairwell clamored with the wooden thunder of the oak-paneled armor case tumbling down the rock steps, gaining speed as it bounced.

Wood splintered. Metal rang as long strips of panel began to break loose under the terrific battering. Hinges smashed. And a moment later, Deo Daley's buckskin-clad body was rolling head over heels down the last steep terrace of stone steps, incased in a breaking cage of kindling wood!

Crrunch! At a final ear-rending jar, Deo Daley felt himself skidding into the clear as the deluge of clattering sticks cracked to matchwood against the rock wall of the torture chamber. The mad fall was finished.

The scout got to his feet, lurching like a drunken man. His head was spinning like a top about to wabble off center. The air was thick with billowing silt, glue dust, showering splinters, and flying hinges.

"Kind of a—rough way—to escape—but it worked!" wheezed the frontier scout, rubbing a score of bruises. "Now, where am I?"

An almost dead torch smoked in a wall niche nearby. Deo Daley lurched over to it, picked it up, and fanned it into a blaze.

An exclamation of surprise came from his bruised lips as Daley saw the open door of the treasure vault, across the room. He had rolled down the stairs to where he had started.

The scout of Terror Trail presented a battered appearance as he stood there, his dazed mind unable to figure things out.

His brown hair was matted with blood. His cleancut, handsome features were bruised and gashed from his hard tumble.

A cartridge belt girdled his waist, but the holster at his thigh was empty. And that fact told Deo Daley that Curt Thode, after knocking him out from behind, had disarmed him. Sick with fear, Daley staggered to the plunder room.

"Irene! Tex! Where are you?" The scout's choked cry of alarm echoed back mockingly from the empty treasure chamber. The flickering blaze of his torch reflected back off caskets filled with glittering jewels, off bars of gold and stacks of tarnished money.

His heart suddenly jelled with a clammy horror, as he turned and sprinted hard for the stairs. As he limped up the stone steps, Daley thought of the terrible things that might have happened to his two companions during the time he had been out.

"I'm a double-decked blockhead for lettin' Curt Thode lay for me!" snarled the scout of Terror Trail, as he vaulted over the scattered armor on the landing.

"Thode was braver than I thought, I guess—"

A crash of gunfire spurred Daley's steps as he raced out into the courtyard of the Alcazar. He was in time to see the foremost of the outlaw mob crawl out of the water-filled moat and head for the door of the castle wall.

"Deo! Deo! Up here, son!" At the same instant, the gunfire lulled and Deo Daley looked up to see the figure of Tex Garland on the balcony of the castle wall. "Watch out for Thode."

Daley did not know that not a minute before, Irene Garland had plunged through a trapdoor, back in the castle. He supposed she was up on the balcony, with her father.

Brrang! Bullets plucked the fringed leggings of Daley's flying feet as he ducked into the door.

Two minutes later, the scout of Terror Trail was on the balcony, with wide-eyed Tex Garland rushing forward with a smoking six-gun.

"I meant for you to duck back in the castle—Irene's in there, Daley!" yelled the old man. "An' I'm out o' shells—just fired my last one. Cain't keep them skunks from gettin' in now."

The color rushed from Daley's face as he sprang to the balcony wall and saw the plaza below swarming with crooks. At the same instant, the crooks spotted the two men on the balcony above them, and rushed for the doorway in the wall below like a pack of wolves.

"Quick—we must try an' join Irene by another door across on the opposite wall!" snapped Daley, thumbing .45 bullets from his belt and cramming them in Garland's fingers. "Otherwise, we'll be trapped

164

inside o' this wall—be cut off from gettin' to Irene—"

But they were already too late. Even as Daley and Garland reached the hallway, they saw the narrow door blocked with half-naked Apache savages and bearded renegades, howling for murder.

"They've got us, Tex! Hurry—dive through this door!"

Bullets roared out of the gloom. Six-guns spat flame. Smoke clouds blossomed like white flowers. With their lives hanging in the balance, Deo Daley and Tex Garland leaped into a doorway at their sides. They found themselves in a tiny, stone-walled room.

Daley's fingers groped for and found the oaken bar which locked the slab doorway. Even as he slid it home in its slot in the stone door casing, the thick panels jolted under the crash of driving shoulders. Outside, the roaring mob of outlaws were sliding to a stop, triggering bullets into the thick door.

"They've—got us trapped for sure, now!" gasped Garland, as the ancient door shook on its hinges. He ejected empties from his .45, reloaded with steady fingers. "There's a window, Daley—let's light a shuck out o' here. That door'll bust any minute!"

Deo Daley grinned his fighting grin, shook sweat out of his eyelashes, and leaped across the tiny room to the loophole window which pierced the thick wall of masonry. He looked out, and his face was suddenly drained of color.

The window opened on a sixty-foot drop to the hard, rocky earth below. They were trapped inside one of the overhanging turrets of the castle, with a rage-maddened mob of outlaw killers already starting to demolish the door in their faces!

IRENE'S FATE

BEFORE IRENE GARLAND could realize the fact that she had been dropped through a trap in the castle floor, she was falling downward in the midst of a shower of rifles, six-guns, and knives, which she had been carrying to assist her father in defending the castle.

The fall lasted twenty feet, and ended in a drenching splash. Water and the soft, silty bottom of an underground tunnel cushioned the impact of her landing.

Struggling to her feet in oozy sludge which mounted above her ankles, Irene found herself in pitch blackness, and with sour-odored water coming to the level of her waist. The guns had vanished beneath the inky water.

"What—what happened?" gasped the girl, reeling unsteadily on her feet, and placing both palms to her temples.

As her eyes became accustomed to the blackness, Irene saw that her lot was not so bad as it seemed. Her first thought was that possibly she had stumbled into a cistern. If so, her fate would be far more horrible than being shot.

But now, her eyes caught a faint, gray wash of light, which traced a little lane of ghostly pin points, dancing along the surface of a long corridor of water.

"I know! This is one of the sewers that Don Picadero built under his castle!" gasped the girl. "The trapdoor I fell through was used to drop our scraps down."

As a matter of fact, the tunnel into which she had

166

fallen in so strange a manner was the water supply system which Don Picadero had installed, and not a sewer. At one time, the water was kept fresh and moving, because it tapped the Rio Torcido, but the channel had long since become plugged with debris, so that it was now stagnant and poisonous.

The hole through which Irene had plunged was the trapdoor where the ancient Spaniards had lowered buckets, to obtain water for cooking, washing, or drinking. It had been the combined weight of Irene and her load of heavy firearms that had finally budged the ancient stone pivots, holding the trapdoor.

Tugging her booted feet out of the gummy slime, Irene commenced wading toward the far-off glimmer of light. An instant later, her forehead brought up sharp against the stone ceiling.

A throbbing welt grew on her brow as she stooped, and continued to slosh her way forward. Her head rubbed against the dank, moldy top of the sewer channel. Her feet slogged through mud six inches deep, which had collected under the stagnant water.

The stench of the tunnel, thick with foul air, made a feeling of nausea attack her stomach. But she struggled on, splashing her way yard by yard, through light that was growing steadily brighter. This indicated an opening, somewhere ahead.

Her muscles ached. Her spine seemed to bear her down, but the tube was scarcely four feet in diameter, and two-thirds filled with mucky, ink-black water.

Suddenly the girl found another opening above her, and with a gasp of joy, she looked upward, to see the iron rungs of a rusted ladder mounting a shaft overhead into a room of the Alcazar above.

Gripping the scaly ladder with cold-numbed hands,

Irene drew herself out of the water and climbed stiffly until she had her head at the level of a floor. Glancing about the gloomy room, she recognized it, with a gasp of relief, as the kitchen of the castle.

But even as the girl started to draw her body from the hole, she stopped, paralyzed with horror.

Into the dimly lighted kitchen stalked two towering Apaches, their faces hideous with war paint, their half-naked bodies glinting dully in the gloom!

Irene stifled a gasp of terror, and lowered herself swiftly back into the opening. Clinging to the wet iron bars of the ladder, she cringed with a pounding heart while she heard the two Indians above go groping about the kitchen, muttering savagely.

"They must be—looking for Daddy!" The thought flashed through Irene Garland's mind. "They'll find me here, sure!"

Without a hint of sound, Irene lowered herself until her boots sank once more into the stale water. Releasing her grip on the ladder, the girl ducked under the ceiling of the sewer channel and waded silently out from under the opening above.

She had hardly done so before one of the feathered Apaches above dropped on hands and knees at the edge of the opening, and peered down into the depths with grunts of disappointment. They had sneaked into the kitchen in search of food, not captives.

"I can't stay in this water—I'll freeze!" gasped the girl, shuddering. "And I've got to get out there to Daddy. I wonder—"

As she turned about, her eyes met a half moon of light—an outside opening of the tunnel, just visible around a square corner. Through the exit, Irene could see a flat floor of ripple-wrinkled water, ending against a grass-hung bank thick with crusty lily pads.

"The moat!" gasped Irene, understanding at last. "This tunnel connects with the moat outside."

Two minutes later, she had waded the twenty feet to the opening and found her body sliding into the depths of the moat which girdled the Castle of Thieves.

Seconds afterward, Irene Garland was dragging herself out on the bank, and was filling her lungs with the first fresh air she had breathed since the trapdoor had plunged her into the tunnel.

For a moment, she stood shivering, struggling to collect her spinning senses and form a plan of action. Suddenly, she turned stiff as a statue, as a familiar cry reached her ears:

"Irene! Irene! Mebbe you can help us!"

Irene voiced a cry, and stared about her, right and left. Then she let her eyes follow up the mossy gray expanse of the stone wall which towered for sixty feet above her.

There, head and shoulders hanging out of a slotlike loophole in the overhanging turret sixty feet above her head, was Deo Daley, waving his arms madly to attract her attention!

"Quick, Irene—run out to our horses an' get a couple o' lariats!" shouted the scout of Terror Trail, as Irene ran back away from the castle, so she could peer up at the turret window. "They got us trapped in here, an' we can't jump! Hurry!"

Shaking her head with bewilderment, opening her mouth to shout words that would not come, Irene obeyed Daley's wildly pointing arms. She ran out across the green meadow to where their horses were grazing on the lush grass.

Risking possible discovery from outlaws who might

be outside the castle, the frontier girl ran to Gunpowder, Daley's coal-black mustang, and removed his thirty-foot picket rope. From her father's line-back dun, grazing nearby, she untied a forty-foot rawhide lariat.

She knotted the two ropes together and coiled them over her arm as she sprinted back toward the castle. As she ran, she saw the reason why Deo Daley and her father could not dive from the turret room into the moat below. The overhanging turret placed the window of their prison room out over the bank, where such a long drop would be fatal.

"Tie a rock in the hondo an' whirl it like a sling shot, savvy?" came Daley's shout, as the girl came to a halt below the turret. "An' hurry—they're about to batter this door down. Your dad an' I can't hold out much longer."

Her father, then, was alive and safe! At least, safe if she could get Daley's daring plan into operation. She realized that their escape from death rested in her hands.

Pulling a slimy rock out of the moat bank, Irene proceeded to tie the stone into the lariat rope. Then she backed away, laying the coil of rope on the ground at her feet. Spinning the rope over her shoulders like a sling shot, she prepared to throw the rock-weighted end of the rope upward toward Daley's window.

Deo Daley was thankful that Irene Garland was a muscular outdoor girl. She could throw a rock like a man. And it was no small trick, throwing a rock sixty feet in the air!

Four times, the scout of Terror Trail reached out to snatch at the rock. But each time, he was forced to pull himself back on the window sill to keep his balance.

Each failure meant a breath-taking delay, while Irene recoiled the rope.

But on the fifth throw, Daley seized the rope as the girl's makeshift sling shot carried it upward past the window.

Minutes later, Irene Garland stood back with tears of relief streaming down her bronzed cheeks, and watched her aged father crawl backward out of the window and inch his way down the rope which hung from the turret to the ground below.

Then she was in her father's arms, and Deo Daley, having lashed the rope inside the turret, was sliding hand-over-hand downward until his moccasin-clad feet touched the welcome security of the grass below. Irene's steady nerves had saved them both from death.

"What are we goin' to do now, Daley?" gasped Tex Garland, running spread-out fingers through his thatch of graying hair. "The inside o' the castle is swarmin' with crooks."

Deo Daley hitched up his belt and peered anxiously at the window above, from which dangled their rope. Faintly to their ears came the smashing of shattered wooden timbers.

"They must a gotten hold o' some of those Spanish battleaxes, an' are choppin' the door down," clipped the frontier scout tensely. "An' when they get inside, they'll discover we've escaped. So the thing for us to do is get out o' this crater hole while the gettin' is good. We can't even take time to catch our horses."

Like three scared rabbits, the adventurers of Terror Trail made their way out across the grassland toward the spot where the Rio Torcido, after winding its way across the bottom of the crater hole, finally tunneled its way through the only means of escape.

171

"Doesn't it make you mad, havin' to dust out o' here an' leave the *Alcazar de los Ladrones* in Curt Thode's hands?" panted the scout of Terror Trail, as the three halted on the bank of blue shale which flanked the mouth of the cavern. "We'll be damned lucky if we can get back to civilization an' the settlements without leavin' our bones on Destruction Desert. Maybe we can kill a deer with that six-gun. An' all the while, Thode an' his skunks will be gettin' the gold an' usin' this castle for a hide-out."

Bitterness and despair welled in the hearts of the three as they edged their way to the bank, preparing for the icy plunge into the gentle current of the river, which would carry them through that foaming tunnel to the safety of La Crescenta Canyon.

"How did you get out o' that castle, Irene?" demanded Tex Garland suddenly. "Things have happened so quick I ain't even asked you where all the guns are—an' why you're drippin' wet."

While the two men stood panting beside her, Irene Garland explained her unexpected plunge through the trapdoor of the Castle of Thieves, her long wade through the underground sewer tube to the kitchen where she had narrowly missed being captured by the Indians, and her eventual exit to the outdoors.

As she finished speaking, Deo Daley seized her deerskin-clad shoulder, and shot an eager question at the girl:

"You say that sewer had an opening in the kitchen, huh? The one we threw the garbage down after we cooked our meals yesterday?" demanded the scout of Terror Trail, his eyes suddenly narrowing in thought. "Listen, folks. We've *got* to have food, if we're goin' to cross Destruction Desert an' reach the settlements

172

alive.

"So you two wait here, savvy? I'm goin' back to that castle, swim through the sewer Irene escaped out of, get into the kitchen an' grab some food together.

"Then I'll be back, an' join you here—maybe after dark, so's they won't see me. You two get out into La Crescenta Canyon."

Irene gasped in alarm at the scout's plan. "But, Deo, that castle is full of crooks!"

Daley turned to the old man, his eyes as bright and hard as polished nailheads, his mouth set with determination.

"Listen, Tex. Get Irene an' you out into the canyon outside. I'll get some food an' join you as soon as I can."

Irene shook her head, and clung to Daley's arm. "No, Deo—let's not risk it. They'd only capture you."

Deo Daley gently removed her two hands from his sleeve. A dogged grin creased his handsome features. "But we have to have food, Irene," he reminded her softly. "We'd starve out on the desert. An' I promise you, I won't take any foolish chances—like gettin' revenge on Curt Thode or tryin' to get some o' that treasure. Revenge an' gold aren't as valuable as gettin' the three of us back to civilization again."

Before the girl could cry out again, the scout of Terror Trail had stooped to kiss her, and then he was gone, over the grassy hummock which loomed between the mouth of the exit cave and the castle.

The two Garlands paled with fear, and then crept through the grass to the top of the knoll, and watched while they saw the daring young scout of Terror Trail slip back across the meadow until he came to the moat.

173

Seconds later, they saw him turn, wave a farewell, and then dive into the scummy water. Soon his swimming figure vanished into the black mouth of the sewer drain through which Irene had escaped, only a few moments before.

"He—he shouldn't have taken that chance, Daddy!" sobbed the girl, giving away at last to her emotions. Tex Garland's seamed face etched with hard lines, as he led his daughter back to the blue shale bank of the river.

"Don't worry about Daley," consoled the old man gently. "After all, we can't travel without grub. The thing for us to do now is git out into La Crescenta an' wait for the scout. He's doin' his share—we got to do ours, Irene."

The girl's shoulders quivered with sobs as she made ready to dive into the river.

"But I love him, Daddy—I love him with all my heart!" choked Irene, as her father took his place beside her. "But let's go!"

The two adventurers, getting their footing for the dive, did not hear a faint rustling sound issue from the black willows near the cavern mouth. The scrubby thicket was directly behind them.

Out through the whippy scrub crept two half-naked figures, from whose lacquer-black hair dangled frowzy eagle feathers. They were Apache warriors, whom Curt Thode had posted there to prevent any possible attempt of their prisoners to escape.

Irene and the old man were poised to dive. But before they could launch their bodies through the air, they felt iron-muscled arms girdle their waists, and they were swept backward away from the river bank and hurled to the earth.

A piercing scream of terror pealed from Irene Garland's throat as red-skinned arms whipped about her like the coils of a snake. Then her cries ceased, as she felt the cold, sharp blade of a hunting knife resting against her throat.

Tex Garland, pinned flat on his back with a leering Apache's knees holding his arms to the grass, was too dazed from the impact of his fall even to pull a cry out of his throat.

"Ugh—we take um to *Señor* Thode!" chuckled the Indian who had caught Irene Garland. "Thode kill um!"

Deo Daley sloshed his way through the sewer tunnel under the *Alcazar de los Ladrones,* until he came to the opening which Irene Garland had mentioned—the shaft leading up through the thick stone floor of the kitchen.

Standing thigh-deep in the slimy water, the scout of Terror Trail held his breath and listened. No sound reached him from the room above. Apparently the Apaches who had so nearly found Irene, had satisfied their hungry stomachs and departed.

Daley quickly spotted the rusty tier of iron ladder rungs, extending up through the circular tube overhead. Testing his weight on the ancient iron bars, the scout swung his body out of the water and climbed the ladder, until his head was level with the kitchen floor.

The room was deserted. But he could hear shouts ringing through the castle, as if from a great distance. The popping of six-guns and the clang of metal made a gruesome undertone.

"That means they've just busted down that turret

door an' have discovered their birds have flown!" chuckled Daley to himself, as he drew his water streaming body out on the kitchen floor and stood up. "That means a gang of 'em will slide down that rope an' will be huntin' out in the meadow for us."

Daley clawed green, mossy slime off his buckskin blouse and disentangled water-grass spears from the copper ornaments of his fringed buckskin leggings. A frown sobered his forehead.

"I hope Irene an' ol' Tex get through the cave into La Crescenta Canyon in time," muttered the young plainsman. "I'll prob'ly have to wait until midnight or so before I can sneak out."

The scout's moccasined feet made no sound as he slipped about the gloom-filled kitchen, assembling a pack load of food from their supplies, which they had stored here. Soon he had assembled enough to last them for their flight across the desert.

Beans, two slabs of bacon, flour and salt. A package of coffee, sugar. For utensils, he grabbed up a soot-blackened frying pan, a butcher knife, tin cups, and a coffee pot. Swiftly, he dumped them into an empty potato sack, and tied it up securely.

As he was in the act of going back into the sewer, Daley heard a sound of shouting outside, and the pealing treble of a woman's voice. And there was only one woman there!

Running to the cobweb-hung slot of window which furnished the kitchen its only light, Deo Daley peered out, to catch a view of the castle's outer gate. And what he saw there robbed his body of its power to move.

Through those outer portals of the Castle of Thieves came two yelling Apaches. And in their arms struggled Irene Garland and her father.

176

Air whistled across Deo Daley's teeth like escaping steam, as he saw Curt Thode plunge out of the castle wall's doorway, followed by the yelling, murderous outlaws who were returning from the job of breaking down the door of the turret room, only to find their prisoners had escaped. Now they had an object to wreak their vengeance upon, and they were quick to grasp the opportunity.

Daley groaned, as he sank back in the shadows of the kitchen. Like a drunken man, he stared across the open courtyard, to see Curt Thode rush forward to where the two gloating redskins held their captives. Then the two Garlands were hidden in the center of a bawling, swearing press of bandits.

"They're done for, this time!" moaned the scout, as he peered through the window slit, his dazed eyes still glued to that jam of gunhung outlaws surrounding his two captured companions.

Curt Thode's fiendish yell lifted above the roar of the mob, silencing them. And the order which the treacherous army officer gave the gang turned Deo Daley's spine into a stick of jelly.

"We'll take 'em down to the torture dungeon where Don Picadero killed *his* captives!" came Curt Thode's shout, harsh as a slap in the face. "An' while they're squirmin' in torture, they'll see us walkin' out o' the treasure chamber loaded down with Spanish gold!"

Weak and suddenly sick, Deo Daley leaned back against the dank, mossy wall and watched with staring eyes as the mob of outlaws trooped through the narrow doorway in the castle wall.

They were taking a helpless old man and a defenseless girl down to the torture machinery that had been transplanted into this house of horror from the days of the Spanish Inquisition. Curt Thode would take no slightest chance of his victims escaping, this time. Daley knew Thode would torture them, in short order.

And watching them die would be Don Chirlo's devilish gang of bandits. Forty of them, at least, all armed to the teeth. What chance had a lone man, without so much as a knife, against such odds?

For the first time in his life, the courageous young scout of Terror Trail admitted crushing, total defeat.

GUILLOTINE

THE NARROW PIT in the bedrock, down which terraced the crumbling stone steps to the dungeon, rang with yells and oaths and booming, triumphant gunfire as Curt Thode led his gang, with their trembling victims, down to the torture den of Don Picadero.

Reaching the chamber of torture, Thode ordered a yellow-bearded outlaw to light a fresh pitch-soaked torch of pine knot, which they had obtained from the trees growing at the foot of the cliffs outside.

Waiting until the ruddy glare of the flames shed its grim witchglow upon the scene, Curt Thode strode over to the door of the treasure chamber, and then turned to his panting mob of crooks.

"An' now, Irene—an' you, Old Man Garland—I got somethin' for you to witness!" taunted the spy, leering into the faces of the two helpless prisoners, who were unable to move a muscle in the grips of the four wiry Apache savages who held them. "Here's what my men have been waitin' so long to see!"

And so, while the two prisoners stared with panic-stricken eyes, Curt Thode strode into the treasure vault. A moment later, he emerged into the light, his palms heaped high with golden money. Guffawing like a madman, Curt Thode flung the handful of gold in all directions.

The coins clanked musically on the stone floor, sending the outlaws and savage Indians to their knees, clawing and scrambling to pick up the rolling treasure.

"You fellers wait here, an' keep those two prisoners close-hobbled," chuckled Thode, striding through the scrambling ranks of men on the floor. "Soon as I get back, we'll start torturin' 'em."

Thode motioned to two Mexican crooks, who stepped forward to his side. Loud shouts of approval were meeting Thode's suggestion. They did not see the crafty gleam which kindled in the traitor's black, hooded eyes as he led the two Mexicans away toward the door of the torture den.

"Upstairs, you two *mozos*," grated Thode in an undertone. "I want you to rope every hoss an' burro that's grazin' up on the pasture. Savvy? We're goin' to start takin' that gold out an' loadin' it on."

The two Mexicans, their eyes snapping, ducked into the darkness and scuttled up the steps, eager to do Thode's bidding. They did not know that Thode was using them as tools to further the plan which he had carefully mapped out in his poisonous brain.

The very gold which he had thrown out, like grain to a flock of starving birds, had been part of the careful stage set designed to keep Chirlo's mob from seeing him put his scheme into operation. For Curt Thode was an expert at the double-cross.

Keeping the mob in the dungeon would be easy, Thode knew. Watching the prisoners, jeering at them, perhaps flogging them with gun belts, would keep them busy. And the treasure vault would be like a magnet attracting iron filings, with that gang!

Moving quickly, Curt Thode sprinted up the steps of the dark dungeon and out into the castle courtyard once more. Then he stopped, remembering something.

"If I'm goin' to make a getaway with all the pack animals loaded with gold, it's a cinch I'm goin' to need grub!" he reasoned. "I'll just run to the kitchen an' scrape together some chow to take with me tonight." The kitchen was empty when Curt Thode entered it. But in the middle of the stone floor was the potato sack which, only ten minutes before, Deo Daley had stuffed with provisions and kitchen utensils, for his own escape!

"Huh! I don't know who did this, but it's sure put up to order!" chuckled Thode, as he examined the contents of the sack and then swung it aboard his shoulder. "Luck's sure breakin' my way!"

Going outside the castle, Thode made his way across the moat by means of a log which the outlaws had rigged up as a bridge. Gaining the opposite bank, the spy made his way out across the grassy basin of the castle's deep, cylinder-shaped pit.

Throaty yells and thudding hoofs, off on the other side of the castle, told Curt Thode that his two Mex vaqueros were busily rounding up the burros and horses, on which the gold would be loaded. Thode chuckled to himself. His scheme was working perfectly.

Night was toiling up out of the east, as the sunset glow burned down to veil the Alcazar de los Ladrones. But a sickle of butter-yellow moon was ramming a horn over the pine-draped rimrocks above, promising a mellow night for Curt Thode's double-cross flight.

A horse was watering itself at the bank of the Rio Torcido, which threaded across the basin. As Curt Thode drew near, his heart leaped with pleasure. It was Gunpowder, the magnificent black mustang belonging to Deo Daley!

"Perfect!" whispered the crook to himself, drawing closer and holding out a hand as the horse threw its head up and blew water from its dripping muzzle. "I been wantin' this hoss for years."

Gunpowder knew Curt Thode, from their days at Fort Adois. It was, therefore, no trick for the Army man to grab the animal's hackamore halter.

Leading the horse to the mouth of the exit cavern, Curt Thode stopped before a heap of canvas-covered packs, where they had been stripped off the burros and dumped. In a moment, he had selected Gunpowder's rig, saddled the horse, and then tied it to a nearby cottonwood scrub. The potato sack filled with food he carefully lashed to the cantle.

"There! You'll be waitin' for me when I'm ready to high-tail it out o' here tonight!" chuckled the outlaw spy, clapping his palms together in a gesture of satisfaction. "An' now to do the important part o' preparin' a getaway."

Curt Thode realized that if he attempted to get away with the gold-laden pack train that night, pursuit would be sure. But he had a plan to block that possibility—a plan he had been evolving in his head all day.

The food packs of the expedition, including those which Chirlo's gang had stolen from Deo Daley's outfit, had been transported inside the Castle of Thieves. But these packs held the various tools, bed

181

rolls, and other equipment, both of the outlaw gang and Daley's party. On his findings here depended the success of Thode's scheme.

"If I remember right, Don Chirlo carried a case o' dynamite with 'im, in case he ran across any gold-bearin' rock durin' his travels in the badlands," muttered Thode to himself, as he took out a knife and slit open pack after pack by slashing the ropes. "Right now, that dynamite's goin' to turn up more yellow gold for me than ever before in the history o' the hoot owl trail!"

If anyone had watched Thode's movements next, he would have been puzzled. But the Mex peons were busy roping the stray burros, and the gang was down deep in the treasure dungeons.

Moving like a shadow in the gathering dusk which was pooling like purple ink in the bottom of the deep, cliff-walled pit, Curt Thode pawed through the heap of packs until he uncovered one which was a wooden box.

In the dim light, he made out two words in red paint: *Danger—Explosive.* The spy's teeth gleamed in a snarling chuckle as he pulled off a board from the lid of the box, and rummaged his hand through the sawdust which it contained.

The case was nearly filled with dynamite sticks, used for blasting purposes by the dead Don Chirlo and his gang, whenever they came across "gold sign" in the rocks of the wastelands.

In the same pack, Curt Thode found a box containing a coil of fuse and a package of dynamite caps. He carefully fitted one cap to the fuse, buried the cap deep in the box, and clamped down the wooden lid once more, leaving the fuse extending outside.

Next, Thode obtained a pick and shovel from the

tarpaulin-bound pack of prospecting tools belonging to Tex Garland.

The growing darkness masked Curt Thode's movements as he proceeded to shovel out a shallow hole in the blue shale upthrust which flanked the mouth of the Rio Torcido's cavern. That done, he cautiously picked up the dynamite case, carried it to the hole, and then scooped over it several inches of shale.

After throwing the pick and shovel into the river, Thode carried a square canvas tarp to the loose mound of blue shale covering his dynamite plant, and carefully spread it out in such a way as to cover the several feet of fuse leading to the explosive.

"There! After I light the fuse, they won't see it sputterin'—in case they start followin' me too soon," chuckled the crook, as he headed back for the Castle of Thieves. "An' by the time they shovel away the dirt that'll block the cavern, I'll be out in the hills with the gold where they'll never discover me."

Thode waited at the moat until his two Mexican cowboys led before the castle portal a string of four horses and eight burros, tied together with lariats. Thode grinned, and patted the two sombreroed killers on the back.

"'*Sta bueno,* amigos!" he complimented. "Picket those animals, an' then we'll be gettin' down to that torture den an' finish off the gal an' her father!"

Deo Daley had paused only a few moments in the kitchen of the Castle of Thieves. He was not the type to give up to despair; instead, he quickly decided to take the suicidal risk of following Curt Thode and his outlaws down to the torture chambers.

"I'll go out to the castle's lobby room an' see if I

can find a gun!" decided the scout of Terror Trail, as he hurried through the empty halls. "If I could put a bullet through Curt Thode's noggin before he does his dirty work—"

A thorough search of the huge central banquet hall, or lobby, of Picadero's Alcazar resulted in nothing. Evidently Irene had made a thorough job of picking up their firearms, before she had been dumped into the secret trapdoor in the floor.

Frantic, the scout headed for the stair which would lead him down to the dungeon. He heard steps preceding him, but in the darkness he did not see that it was Curt Thode and his two Mexican helpers, returning from their work outside.

"Gosh! They'll mow me down flat if I try to sneak down there in these clothes!" panted the desperate scout, looking down at his red-striped trousers. "What in hell am I goin' to do?"

Suddenly, Daley came to the landing where had stood the armor chest in which he had been placed by Curt Thode. Still scattered about the landing, kicked back in the corners by the slogging feet of the mob, were the remnants of silvery Spanish armor.

From below came the murmur of many voices, and then a girl's piercing screams. The horde below were welcoming Curt Thode back to the torture den, little knowing of the fiendish double-cross job he had been doing outside.

Again the girl's scream, and her cry settled the suicidal decision which had corkscrewed into Deo Daley's brain. A desperate, absurd chance, but risk meant nothing to the scout of Terror Trail, now. To be near Irene in her last moments was all that counted.

Stooping, Deo Daley snatched up the heavy coat of

chain mail which lay at his feet. The steel links were heavy, but he found the sleeves and wriggled into the coat. With forty pounds of linked metal over his buckskin blouse, his movements were retarded; but it would make an effective disguise, and such was the scout's plan in donning the Spaniard's armor.

"If anybody comes out while I'm goin' down the steps, I'll just lie down an' they'll think I'm another one o' those armored skeletons that's scattered around this castle," panted Daley, as he groped about to pick up a set of steel breastplates which he buckled over the tinkling meshes of the looped armor. "There's several armored skeletons down in the torture den, so maybe I can pass for one."

He started violently as the sound of Curt Thode's voice wafted up the stairwell to smite his eardrums: "Start packin' out this gold, you hombres! We ain't puttin' the gal or the old man on the torture machines until you got those pack bosses loaded outside! We're all movin' out o' here tomorrow mornin' an' we'll divide the treasure out in Destruction Desert!"

Daley snatched up the ancient, silver-plated Spanish helmet. He adjusted it over his head, lifted the hinged visor on its creaky joints, and peered about. The armor had kept in fairly good condition through the centuries. No doubt it had been a prized suit of fighting clothes, else it would not have been carefully oiled and polished and put away.

The scout found a pair of glittering steel-plate gloves, which bristled with spiked points at the knuckles. But he laid them aside. No use cluttering up his hands with this grim disguise.

Shin plates and a skirtlike affair of chain-ring mail were littered about the stairway below, to complete the costume of a knight. But fresh screams of Irene Garland brought dew out like a mist on the scout's brow, and he headed down the stairs, chain mail tinkling softly.

What a desperate masquerade! A frontier scout, wearing buckskins and a cartridge bandoleer beneath the glittering armor of a long-dead pirate of the Spanish Main!

It was the queerest, weirdest role a man had ever played. But Deo Daley was afire with desperation, as he stole down those haunted steps and set foot on the floor of the torture chamber.

Footsteps sounded. Advancing shadows wagged around the corner which shut off the mob from Daley's view. Someone was coming!

Daley dropped flat on his stomach. The creaky helmet visor snapped shut, masking his face. But as he lay there, Deo Daley could see through the slitted eye-holes. And around the corner of that stonewalled room came two Apaches and a white outlaw, backs bent under the burden of boxes laden with jewels!

The outlaw's high-heeled boots clattered inches from Deo Daley's face. But the three treasure-burdened outlaws passed on up the stairs, little dreaming that a living person breathed inside those steel breastplates, that a pair of slitted eyes burned behind the slotted visor of that ancient Spanish helmet!

The outlaws had seen many a twisted, mummified corpse, clad in rusty armor, scattered about the courtyard, the corridors, the walls and dungeons of this amazing lost castle. If they noticed Daley's prostrate form at all in the black shadows, they passed it off as another one of the skeletons who had fallen, clothed in armor, about the Castle of Thieves three centuries before.

As soon as the outlaws had passed out of sight up the stairs, Daley was on hands and knees, scuttling around the corner of the torture den and into the shadow of a grim torture rack. Again he flattened, as three more outlaws filed out, arms laden with gold ingots like sticks of stove wood.

Through a rift in the jam of outlaws who were streaming out of the treasure chamber with their golden burdens, Daley could see Irene and Tex Garland, standing in hopeless dejection in the grips of their Apache captors. Nearby, the straw-bearded torchbearer kept the blazing knot aloft, to light the chamber. There followed a quarter of an hour of agonizing waiting, which planted the seeds of many a gray hair in Deo Daley's scalp. He knew he could not afford to be seen moving, or he would be gunned down by a startled outlaw.

So, step by step, he made his way through the darker corners of the torture chamber, unseen by the outlaws who marched in and out of the castle, stripping the treasure vault of its gold and jewel booty and carrying it up to the waiting pack train outside.

Daley himself did not know exactly what to do. At no time were more than half the outlaws outside, going up the stairs. A vague plan was forming in his head that perhaps he could seize a moment when Thode was inside the vault, dash in and club him to unconsciousness, and use him as hostage to dicker for the safety of Irene and Tex Garland.

But then, he decided, the crooks liked Thode no better than he did, perhaps. They were obeying his orders only because they were drunk with the sight of the treasure.

And then the last of the outlaws filed out of the now

empty treasure vault, and Daley's stomach crawled as he realized his last chance was gone. Already, the den was filling with returning outlaws. The curtain was about to rise on the torture of their victims, and not a bandit in the horde wanted to miss the show.

Curt Thode, standing full in the glare of the torch, held up his hands for silence as the last of the treasure carriers returned from the outdoors.

"An' now, *amigos*," announced the spy, like a ringmaster about to introduce the main spectacle of the circus, "you're goin' to see this pretty gal here die like a real castle queen should die. In the old days, they used to behead queens. An' there's a beheadin' machine right here, gang—a genuine guillotine!"

Daley seemed to freeze at the rumble of thunderous approval which followed Thode's awful words. The traitor swung about, and pointed to a large oak-wood frame on top of which was suspended, by two chains running through wooden pullies, a steel blade three feet wide and ten inches high, as thick as a man's wrist.

This blade, now speckled with rust but still as sharp as an ax, was fitted to run down between the two upright wooden timbers which were grooved to take the edges of the thick blade.

At the bottom of the two uprights was a wooden crosspiece like the threshold of a door. A half-circle was sawed from its center, upon which the victim's neck was placed. A set of ring bolts on the stone floor below the beheading engine was fitted with rusty iron bands designed to hold down the victim's body.

"This is the cleverest torture machine in Picadero's bunch," guffawed Curt Thode, stepping forward and walking behind the guillotine. "Watch, you hombres, an' I'll show you how it works."

Irene and Tex Garland, out in front of that sweating half-circle of outlaws, stared in open-jawed terror as they saw Curt Thode point to the steel chains holding the beheading blade aloft.

"These two chains run down here to this trigger board, which is just like the trigger of a big mouse trap," explained Curt Thode, his black eyes snapping venomously. "We'll bolt the girl to the floor, with her neck in this board. Her head will rest up on this trigger. So long as she can keep her head up off the floor, she's all right. But when she gets tired an' lets her head rest down—*powie!* See what'll happen, *amigos*?"

So saying, Curt Thode reached down and touched a trigger board, or headrest, lightly with his finger tips. There sounded a sharp snap as the trigger catch released. Chains rasped through wooden pullies. With a rush of air, the suspended blade above dropped down through its grooves in the upright wooden timbers.

Crrrash! The blade landed with a quivering thud in the wooden neck socket below.

The outlaws paled as they saw Curt Thode seize the chains and attempt to lift the heavy blade. Strong though the traitor was, he could barely lift one end of the blade out of the base block.

"Help me out, here!" commanded Thode. Two brawny, black-whiskered ruffians leaped forward, and tugged their weight on the twin chains fastened to the steel blade.

Hauling it up through its grooved frame until it was once more suspended at the top of the rack, they held the one-hundred-pound blade until Curt Thode could once more set the trigger catch.

Then, while Irene found her voice at last and

screamed in mortal terror, Curt Thode proceeded to fasten the horror-stiffened girl upon the stone floor. Her arms and ankles were clamped by the iron bands, so that she could not move. The back of her neck rested neatly in the half-circle carved out of the back.

Sweat was raining out of Daley's pores. Desperately, he glanced about him, as he lay flat on his face back in the shadows behind the guillotine rack. If he only had a weapon—

Irene Garland felt beneath her head the slight touch of the trigger rest. An ounce of pressure, and it would release that grim blade hanging above her.

She tried to force her eyes shut, but could not. Six feet over her bare, pulsing throat, that wicked giant's razor was suspended, waiting to crash down its grooved slots and sever her head from her body. But that would not come until her neck muscles gave way, and let her head sag down upon the hair-trigger board.

She felt consciousness ebbing. Pure instinct fought to keep her from fainting. The second she relaxed, her head would lower and that heavy blade would crash down toward its chopping block!

Curt Thode grinned like a demon as he stood up and surveyed his work, after locking Irene Garland securely.

Any schoolchild has lain down on the floor and then lifted his head off the rug, to see how long his neck muscles can keep his scalp off the floor. Any child knows how the cords and tendons of the neck begin to ache, until finally all control of the muscles is lost and the head sinks down. Five minutes is the limit for most . . .

Already, Irene Garland's neck muscles were taut with exertion. Her lips worked, but she could not scream her terror. Not when her chin was jamming against her throat, in her effort to keep her skull off that fatal trigger!

"What'll we do with the old man, boss?" questioned one of the outlaws, and Curt Thode took his fascinated gaze away from the panting girl on the floor below, to look at Tex Garland.

The old man was fighting like a maniac, snapping at his guards with his teeth and wrenching every muscle in his body. But he was powerless to throw off the clutches of four burly guards. His face was shiny with sweat. His eyes stared wildly.

"Hang onto 'im—let 'im watch his daughter die!" snarled the cruel traitor, laughing. "Then he gets the same dose!"

The infinite cruelty of the treacherous cavalry lieutenant from Fort Adios came to the fore, now that he had control of the bandit gang. His grating laugh cut Garland's eardrums, as he slumped back, chest heaving.

"Listen, gang!" shouted Thode once more. He knew that the time was now ripe to spring the last part of his double-cross plans. "As soon as these two are croaked, we'll break out all o' Don Chirlo's liquor. An' we'll all get sousin' drunk—the biggest celebration this castle ever seen!"

Yells roared out from the mob. Curt Thode turned his head back to watch the girl, and to keep his men from seeing the crafty gleam which had kindled in his snakish eyes. When those men were drunk, he would make his getaway. And with that dynamite set-up to delay pursuit—it was a cinch.

Deo Daley, back in the gloom, was inching his way closer and closer to the guillotine. The blond-bearded ruffian with the torch moved over beside the beheading rack, the better to light the show of torture. His shadow helped hide Daley's crawling progress.

As he got closer to the grim guillotine, Daley proceeded to wriggle out of his coat of mail, first unsnapping his heavy breastplate s. He could not afford to drag that weight with him, when he made his twofisted attack on Curt Thode. All he could hope for, now, was to kill Thode. The Garlands were doomed.

Closer and closer he crawled, keeping behind the blot of shadow caused by the straw-haired torch bearer. He could not drag his eyes away from Irene, who weltered in her own icy sweat, struggling to keep her scalp away from that fatal trigger board.

Daley was within six feet of Irene's head, unnoticed back in the murk. Thode was edging about, to be closer to the beheading rack when the girl's resistance faltered and doom came.

"If he comes six feet closer, I'll heave this coat o' chain mail at 'im!" panted the scout to himself, wadding the forty pounds of linked steel rings into a compact bundle. "It ought to bowl 'im over—an' once I trigger a slug in his belly I won't care—"

Thode, eyes glued to Irene's sweat-watered face, was edging to a stop beside the straw-haired outlaw who held the guttering torch aloft. With his heart hammering against his ribs, the scout of Terror Trail drew back his arms to launch that heavy ball of rings.

"Goodby—daddy—darling!" It was Irene's choked voice.

For weary, ageless minutes the instinctive love of life in her tortured soul had kept her head erect off that trigger board. But now, with all hope gone, she saw at last the futility of prolonging her torture for the gloating pleasure of Curt Thode and his ruffians.

Her scream was a groan of despair and a wail of farewell at the same time. Then her head relaxed on the headrest board.

There was a sharp snap as the hair trigger was released. Sudden silence seemed almost to explode in the torture chamber for a clipped fraction of a clock tick. Rasping chains jangled through wooden pullies. And the heavy guillotine blade swooshed downward in its grooved slots above the pulsing throat of Irene Garland!

TERROR TRAIL'S END

DEO DALEY HELD in his hands the wadded-up ball of heavy chain armor, which he had been in the act of hurling at Curt Thode's head. Now, with his arms already casting the forty-pound bundle of linked metal rings, he saw the flashing blade start downward on its plummeting journey of death.

Pure instinct swerved the scout's arm muscles downward and to one side. *Wham!* The huge bundle of metal thudded to a chinky landing, square on the block under that dropping blade!

Crrunch! The heavy steel sheared through two inches of the ball of chain links, as an ax might cleave into a wad of soft wood. But the big ball of rolled-up chain armor was not to be cleft.

With a grinding screech, the beheading razor chiseled to a dead stop. One edge was wedged deeply into the heavy ball of metal on the chopping block. And it held the rusted edge of that blade a scant inch away from Irene Garland's paralyzed throat!

All that, the scout of Terror Trail saw in the space

193

of batting an eyelash. Then his rushing dive carried him past the rack and his helmeted head bowled over the startled yellow-beard who was holding the red torch of flaming pinewood.

Whiz! The blazing torch smashed Curt Thode's whirling head square in the eyes.

His yelp of pain gave way to a hoarse bellow of fear as he saw the scout of Terror Trail charge over the blond giant's falling body, to launch a flying tackle at Thode's body.

Deo Daley's shoulder swept Thode to the floor and a whizzing fist turned the army man's nose into a bloody pulp. Curt Thode was crashed on his back at the feet of the outlaws, who were staring in popeyed amazement at the spectacle of a raging demon who had sprung out of nowhere, like a thunderbolt.

A demon with the yellow-striped blue trousers of a Fort Adios cavalry scout, but whose head was incased in a silver Spanish helmet!

Thode bounced to his feet, his hand blurring to his left-hand holster. His fingers clamped about the red pipestone butt of the six-gun which belonged to Deo Daley himself. Steel glinted in a lightning swift draw. Then Thode was jerking the trigger.

Brram! A lance of ragged fire spat from the gun's muzzle, square in the scout's helmeted face, as Daley rushed.

The silver-plated steel helmet was only a tin toy when it came to combating modern firearms. But it saved Deo Daley's life, in that paralyzed instant of stopped time when clouding gunpowder shot in through the slotted helmet visor, stinging his eyeballs. The helmet clanged like a firebell, as it deflected the bullet. The slug chugged into the rising body of the

194

yellow-bearded torchbearer behind Daley. So rapid had been the action that the crook, butted down by the scout's first attack, was just bouncing to his feet when the glancing bullet smashed the brains from his skull.

"It's showdown, Thode!" came out of Daley's helmet.

Thode howled in panic as he felt Deo Daley's fingers close like steel clamps on his wrists. Before the spy could pull back the knurled hammer of the singleaction .45, he felt the bone-crushing pressure squeeze the six-gun from his grasp.

In the twinkling of a gun flash, Deo Daley flipped his red-stocked Colt on the trigger guard, palmed it, and thumbed a bullet into the forward rush of outlaws who had finally broken their spell.

A second gun leaped from a crossdraw holster in Thode's belt. He swept it upward under the scout of Terror Trail's face. The barrel came in line, and the two men faced each other across a twenty-inch void of gun smoke, their eyes blazing with the hatred of enemies who have come to the last desperate showdown.

Spang! At point-blank range, Deo Daley's pipestone-butted Peacemaker roared out its song of death.

A red fountain spurted from a great slot in the middle of one of Curt Thode's black sideburns.

Bang! Another six-gun bullet punched a gushing crater in the center of Curt Thode's sloping, satanic brows.

Bam! And Daley's third cartridge swept the evil Fort Adios traitor to the floor, the leaden missile ripping his treacherous heart asunder . . .

Moving like a phantom, Deo Daley raced through purling gun smoke to shoot down the stubborn guards who still held Tex Garland, a dazed witness to the showdown play. Wounded, one of the screaming Apaches lunged forward with a flashing knife blade, stabbing hard.

But the steel rang harmlessly off Daley's dented Spanish helmet as the scout ducked, then clubbed the savage down with his empty, smoking six-gun.

"Hands up high, everybody! I'll drill the first one who moves!"

A forest of arms sprouted above the gasping mob of men. But Deo Daley knew he could not hope to keep these ruffians at bay more than a few precious seconds, at most.

He holstered his own empty weapon. His hands shot out and stripped two loaded .44s from a pasty-faced Mexican's holsters. The twin guns weaved over the outlaw horde, promising quick death.

"Hold your head tight, Irene!" screeched Tex Garland wildly.

Free of his captors, Tex Garland was a blur of flapping buckskin and bannering whiskers as he leaped to the guillotine and released Irene from her iron bonds. Daley winced with suspense as he saw the old man carefully pull the girl's head from under the heavy blade which was propped up by the wadded ball of chain armor that had saved her life.

"Head for the stairs, Irene! Get goin', Tex! I'll be right up behind you! Grab guns as you go an' shoot to kill!"

An aisle parted in the mob. Grabbing guns from holsters, Tex Garland and his panting daughter made their way out. Bug-eyed, chests heaving, the outlaws were stunned under the threat of six heavy guns holding them in check.

Then the scout of Terror Trail, backing his way

toward the stairs, suddenly turned and bolted like a deer up the steep flight, to follow his two escaping companions.

Confusion broke loose, as the outlaws lowered their arms and charged through the gloom in pursuit of the three prisoners.

The corpse of Curt Thode, grinning wetly through a bloody screen which covered his face, watched the outlaws jam up the stairs. Then he was left alone in death, among the torture engines of an ancient Spanish buccaneer.

Soon the last flame of the torch guttered out on the floor, as the coals were extinguished by the sizzling pool of blood which crawled toward it from Thode's stiffening body . . .

Out of the grim *Alcazar de los Ladrones,* for the last time, sped young Deo Daley. A yowling mob of crooks bayed at his heels, back down the stairs. Like a sprinter, the scout raced out of the castle gates, throwing off his Spanish helmet as he did so.

He reloaded his six-gun as he skittered across the single log which had been thrown over the moat for a bridge span. The scout kicked it into the water to delay his followers.

Through the silvery moonlight which drenched the silent crater, Daley could see the figures of Irene and Tex Garland fleeing to the safety of the exit cavern. Daley grinned, and started after them.

Then he stumbled into a line-back saddle horse— Tex Garland's mount. Daley jerked out the animal's picket pin and vaulted into the saddle, not stopping to figure out why it was saddled. As he swung astride, he noticed that a string of flop-eared burros and other horses were drawn up along the moat, each heavily packed.

"So that's where they've been takin' the treasure!" yelled Daley, gouging hoofs into his saddler's flanks. "We'll get away with part o' Don Picadero's pirate treasure, after all!"

Out across the moonlit grasslands Deo Daley spurred at a dead gallop, just as the first of the outlaws swept out of the castle gates, paused at the moat, then plunged in to swim in vengeful chase.

Saddlebags laden with treasure jounced at Daley's pommel, as he spurred his mount over the grass-carpeted knoll and down to join Irene and Tex Garland on the blue-shale bank beside the exit cavern. Then Daley's jaw dropped open in amazement, as he found his two companions climbing aboard Gunpowder, his own black mustang!

"He was tied here—with a sack o' grub strapped on 'im!" cackled Tex Garland, eyes twin sparks in the moon rays. "I think our gardeen angel must have saddled Gunpowder and given us food."

The mountain crater was choked with echoing gunfire as Daley spurred his horse over the bank into the river.

"Come on!" he yelled, as Gunpowder, carrying double, followed the other horse into the current. "They're right behind us!"

The two horses plunged to the middle of the Rio Torcido and were whisked into the inky maw of the cavern. A split minute later, the foremost of the swearing, roaring army of outlaws plunged like a breaking wave over the knoll in pursuit.

Brrang! A blizzard of useless bullets plucked spray from the river as the baffled outlaws opened a searing volley into the cavern's mouth. And then an incredible thing happened.

One of those streaking, wildly aimed slugs chugged through a spread-out canvas tarpaulin which covered a fresh-spaded mound of blue shale, there on the bank. And then the night ripped wide open.

An explosion rocked the pines on the rimrocks hundreds of feet above. A wall of blinding pink flame swept out to sear the beards of that startled outlaw band. And a geyser of water and bowling rocks erupted in their faces, as if the whole earth were blowing up underfoot.

The weather-eroded cliff wall shook off its outer shell of rock, and a curtain of boulders plunged down in an avalanche. Rocks whistled across the crater and powdered to bits on the turrets and walls of the Castle of Thieves. Smoke palled up to mask the crescent moon.

And when the erupting earth settled back, it completely blocked the mouth of the Rio Torcido's cavern under thousands upon thousands of tons of dislodged rock and dirt.

Curt Thode's devilish dynamite plan had worked far beyond the evil spy's own intentions. The blast had rammed a gigantic stopper into the crater's only door, sealing forever the secret exit of the *Alcazar de los Ladrones!*

"I see you don't realize what that mysterious explosion means to those outlaws," panted Deo Daley, as he and Irene Garland and her grizzled father crawled to safety in La Crescenta Canyon. "See, the river's gone dry behind us. Something blew up back there—I don't know what. But those bandits are bottled up alive. They'll starve or drown before they can possibly shovel their way through."

Irene, beautiful as an angel in the soft moon glow which shed into the canyon, regarded Daley with pity-flooded eyes.

"Drown? You mean they will starve, don't you?"

Daley shook his head, and looked back into the depths of the cave which no longer emitted a river of sudsy water. Now it was only a dripping trickle of foam, which would soon dry up entirely.

"The Rio Torcido will take months to flood that crater, but it will be filled to the brim, sooner or later," responded the scout of Terror Trail, with a wan smile. "The Castle of Thieves will be at the bottom of a mountain lake, then."

Tex Garland was busy rummaging through the potato sack filled with the food and provisions which would enable them to make their way across Destruction Desert to the settlements again.

"While your dad is seein' how much gold we managed to get away with, thanks to Curt Thode's packin' those horses, I want to tell you somethin' personal, Irene!" said the young scout, sliding an arm around the girl's waist. "Seems like I haven't had a breathin' spell to tell you what I been honin' to tell you since—"

Old Tex Garland opened the saddlebags which Thode's men had loaded. The dancing moon rays were shed back at him from a thousand sparkling rubies and diamonds and emeralds, from yellow golden ingots and tarnished Spanish doubloons and English guineas.

They had escaped with only a tiny portion of the Alcazar's staggering total of treasure, but it would be more than enough to keep the three of them in comfort for life.

"Look here, Irene! Just look, Daley. We got—Oh!"

The old man turned his back, and grinned into his salt-gray beard as he looked off through the lilac moonlight . . .

We hope that you enjoyed reading this
Sagebrush Large Print Western.
If you would like to read more Sagebrush titles,
ask your librarian or contact the Publishers:

United States and Canada

Thomas T. Beeler, *Publisher*
Post Office Box 310
Rollinsford, New Hampshire 03869-0310
(800) 818-7574

United Kingdom, Eire, and
the Republic of South Africa

Isis Publishing Ltd
7 Centremead
Osney Mead
Oxford OX2 0ES England
(01865) 250333

Australia and New Zealand

Bolinda Publishing Pty. Ltd.
17 Mohr Street
Tullamarine, 3043, Victoria, Australia
(016103) 9338 0666